Mercy

Kathleen Patrick

For Bob, Ben, and Hanna—for believing in me from the get-go. Your love and support have made all the difference.

mercy: n. kind or compassionate treatment; relief of suffering; kindness in excess of what may be expected or demanded by fairness; forbearance and compassion.

—*Webster's New World Dictionary*

Contents

Spring

August, 1970

Summer

1

When I was twelve years old, my mother got an itch for gambling, and she scratched it more often than she should have. My dad had left three years earlier, disgusted with her and me I guess, and went down to Arizona so he could work construction year round. He left us with the old Volkswagen bus and three months behind on the rent on our small house down by the river. Mother told me that over and over again. Seven-hundred-and-fifty dollars short and divorce papers to boot. I only knew that I was suddenly allowed to stay up late watching movies, and I didn't hear them fighting anymore. Mother got a job at a supper club as a cocktail waitress. That's where she met Wes. Things went along okay for a while, and then he took her to some gambling place across the river. After that, it started to get real messy.

That summer, after I finished the sixth grade, we drove into her brother Charlie's yard, and I knew things were never going to be the same.

Wes drove this old Cadillac that smelled like peppermint air freshener and cigarettes. The seats were dirty tan velveteen. I could still stretch out on that long back seat and sleep; I had been sleeping for hours when we pulled into Charlie's driveway. Mother reached back and shook my knee.

"We're here, Sugarplum. Now wake up."

I was in a thick, deep sleep, and I had a hard time forcing my eyes open. The first thing I saw was a corral with several horses in it. Across from the corral was a small prairie farmhouse with white clapboard siding and dark-green trim on the windows. The grass was long, and dandelions dotted the yard.

A big old cat sat like a statue with its eyes closed next to the cement steps.

"This is it," Mother said. "Seems smaller than I remember."

Out past the house were several small red and white buildings, a tractor, an old pick-up with one front wheel up on a jack, and the barn.

Wes parked the car. "Roll up your windows or the damn flies will be all over in here." He put out his cigarette, reached over Mother to place the keys in the cubbyhole, and glanced at me as he straightened back up. "Sarah Paul, make sure you get all your stuff out of here. Look under the seat too."

Mother shot him a dirty look, and that was the first time I knew there was a major possibility that my mother was going to leave me. Leave me right here on this farm and drive away and not ever, ever look back.

My name is Sarah Paul. Sarah, after my mother's best friend in high school who died in a car wreck her senior year and left my mother totally alone and the saddest girl at her high school graduation. She said life would never be the same, or as good, again. My middle name is Paul after my dad. His name is Paul, and he said he wasn't ever going to have any other kids, and he may as well be remembered somehow, even if I was a mistake and did turn out to be a dumb girl. That's what he said.

So my name didn't exactly make the pride well up inside of me. Mother usually called me Sugarplum for my initials, S. P.. My last name is Sadler, and I told the only two friends I had ever had to call me Sadie, and that worked out just fine.

As I got out of the car that day, I had a strong feeling I wouldn't be seeing those two friends anymore. They lived in my old neighborhood by the river. I didn't figure I'd be seeing that little yellow house again, either. So before I even saw Charlie, I had resigned myself to the idea that my life was taking another turn, and I was headed for a new beginning. I may make it sound easy, but my stomach was in more knots than usual, and I thought that if I didn't concentrate real hard I may throw up, or cry, or both. I looked down at the ground and started stuffing those feelings deep down inside.

Mother knocked on the front door, but no one came right away. Then a guy wearing a cowboy hat and carrying a saddle walked out of the barn. He saw us and walked up toward the house. "Well, look who's here! Hello, sister!" Charlie laid the saddle down on the ground, pushed his beat-up old cowboy hat back on his forehead and put both his hands on his hips. He was a little taller than Wes was and real thin. He had on faded jeans and a blue cotton shirt. His black cowboy boots had long, pointed toes.

"Hi, Charlie. I'd like you to meet my daughter Sarah, and this is Wes, a good friend of mine." Mother's voice sounded tired and almost angry, but she smiled after she finished introducing us.

"This sure is a surprise. I can't say I been expecting no company." Charlie looked from Mother to me to Wes and back to Mother again. He scratched the side of his head. Mother hadn't even talked about her brother much, but I got the impression they weren't exactly close. "Come on in," Charlie said. "I'll put on some coffee." He turned around, chuckling to himself and shaking his head. He left the saddle in the middle of the gravel driveway, opened the screen door and walked inside. When the screen slammed on its spring, all three of us jumped. Mother opened the door and went in after him.

Charlie had never been married. I knew that much from our long car ride. I heard Mother tell Wes that he had been in the Marines for sixteen years, and when he came home all he did was break horses and go on all-day trail rides. Eating, sleeping, drinking and riding horses for about two-and-a-half years. Charlie bought the farm from my grandfather, but then Grandpa died the year before Charlie got out of the Marines.

Then, Mother told Wes, one morning Charlie just decided the long weekend was over; it was time to whip the old farm into shape and start making a living again. After that, he raised and boarded horses and put up the fields in whatever crops seemed to make sense at the time. Mother said something happened in Vietnam that turned Charlie inside out and that he never was the same. Just like when her friend died in that car wreck, I guess. Nothing ever was the same, or as good, again.

Charlie stood over at the counter and put coffee in an electric coffee pot. Next to him stood an old-fashioned stove, the kind you put wood in the bottom for the heat. The whole kitchen looked like something out of an old Walt Disney movie. It was a real mess with open containers and dirty dishes stacked up all over the counters.

Charlie plugged in the coffee pot, then turned and leaned against the counter. He reached into his shirt pocket for a cigarette, squinted while he lit it up and looked at me the whole time. I didn't look down at my feet, but I thought about it. I kept looking right back, thinking maybe he wouldn't like me, and I would get back into that big car after all and drive on to Nebraska or wherever my mother and Wes Knutson decided to go next.

"So how old are you?" Charlie's voice was gravelly, and he wasn't smiling.

"Twelve." I was almost thirteen, but I didn't figure he cared much about that.

"That's old enough to lift a saddle. You ever been riding?"

"No sir," I said, as polite as I knew how. I figured a horse was about the biggest animal I had ever seen up close, and I had no interest whatsoever in climbing up on the back of one.

"Well, if your momma plans to visit for a couple of hours here maybe we'll have to take you out for a little spin. Got a nice little two year old out there. Gentle as a kitten. Wouldn't hurt a fly." Charlie smiled and took a drag from his cigarette. "I call her Mercy." He winked at me, and right then I wasn't afraid of him anymore.

"Sarah Paul, why don't you go outside and look around. I need to talk to your uncle for a bit." Mother raised her eyebrows and motioned toward the door with her head. The look she gave me wasn't half as nice as the one Charlie had given me moments before.

I shrugged. "Here," Charlie said. He handed me a couple of apples. "Go out and introduce yourself to Mercy. She's in the pen by herself out by the barn. The small reddish one with four white socks."

I must have looked confused. "White socks...you know, the white markings around the hooves. They look like socks." Charlie smiled. "Mercy likes apples. Go on. She won't bite. She's a lady. She's got manners."

I took the two apples and didn't say a word. There weren't any words left. Everything I had ever known was stuck in the top of my throat. I couldn't swallow. I couldn't breathe, and I knew as sure as my misfit name was Sarah Paul that my mother was going to try to give me away as soon as the screen door closed, and I was out of listening range. I walked out toward the barn.

The sun was hot in the mid-afternoon sky. I saw dainty, blue flowers growing along the fence. Barn swallows swooped back and forth between the buildings catching bugs. The only sound was a door banging in the breeze somewhere. Tears rolled down my cheeks as I walked toward the horse with four white socks. The tears were quiet and mine alone, but they were the heaviest tears I had ever cried. Each one formed like a lake in my eye before it slid down toward my chin. I saw the horse in a blur. She walked up to the fence; we both reached the wooden boards at the same time. Before I knew it, she reached her long neck over the top board and gently took an apple from my right hand. That left my hand free to wipe at my face. My throat was swollen with fear and longing. I touched the horse's soft nose and waited for words. "Hello, Mercy. My name is Sadie," I finally said.

"Sarah Paul?" Mother walked up behind me. I don't know how long I had been outside, but the sun was a lot farther down in the sky. I was braiding dandelion stems together and had a pile of them sitting next to me. I had stopped crying long ago, and my face was dry. I was glad about that.

"I don't like being called Sarah Paul," I said quietly. "I don't like my name one bit."

Mother sighed and sat down. "Now don't go getting contrary on me, Sarah. This is hard enough for me the way it is." I didn't say anything. I didn't ask any questions. I didn't look her in the eye. I had no intention of making this one bit easier for her. She was about to throw her daughter by the side of the road, and the unbelievable thing, the thing I couldn't get my mind around, was that daughter was me. "Me and your Uncle Charlie have been talking," she said, "and he wondered if you

10

could stay and visit for awhile. You know, to get to know him a little bit. I think he gets lonely out here, and you're his only niece. Some company might do him some good. And besides . . ." Her voice was smooth and natural. Lying came easy to her. "Wes and I are going to be traveling around for awhile, and I know how you don't like long car rides. Then, when I get settled someplace, I can come back and get you. Or maybe you can take a bus."

It was like she was thinking out loud. Making this all up as she went along. I thought I was done crying, but I started shaking and feeling like things were falling apart inside of me. I wrapped my thin arms around my stomach and took a breath. "How long do you expect I'd need to stay here, Mother?"

"I don't know. I need to save us up some money. Raising a kid takes a lot of money. And I have to find a job and get a place to stay." She looked off in the other direction, slowly pushing a strand of hair behind her ear. I decided maybe lying wasn't that easy after all. "He's a good person, Sarah. Charlie does things his own way, that's all. I think you'll like him."

I already missed my mother. Not that we got along all that well the last couple of years. Her staying out so late at night and forgetting to get groceries for my school lunch. Forgetting to wash my clothes. Forgetting to kiss me good night. Forgetting about me all together. But she was the only person in the whole world who knew anything whatsoever about me. I finally turned and looked her in the eye. I wanted to say "I hope you have a good reason for this, Mother," but instead, I smiled my practiced smile and said, "I'll be fine. Just come and get me as soon as you can."

"I will Sugarplum, I will." Mother stood up, brushed off her shorts and smiled over at me. The hard part was over for her, and she knew it. "Wes and I best be getting on the road before it gets much later. Come on in and tell Wes good-bye."

I squinted back toward the house without getting up. "No. I'm not going to tell him anything," I said. Just as I knew I wasn't Sarah Paul anymore, I knew I wasn't about to be nice to that man who was driving my own mother out of my life. "Good-bye, Mother."

She sighed, folded her arms across her chest and looked away. "Okay then, Sassy Pants. At least give your momma a hug." I stood up and let her hug me, but my arms wouldn't do anything I wanted them to. I turned and walked out toward a grove of trees without looking back. Mother never tried to follow me. She never cried. She never called out that she loved me, that she would be in touch, and that she missed me already. She disappeared as soon as my back was turned. I heard the car start up and the tires on gravel as they headed out the driveway. Wes tooted the horn three times. By the time I turned around, all that was left was a lingering cloud of dust hanging over the gravel road that led to the highway.

About ten minutes later, the screen door of the house slammed, and Charlie stepped out. He picked up the saddle from the middle of the driveway and walked out toward the corral. I had settled down against one of the small buildings and was studying a small rock I had been holding since that car drove away with my life. Charlie walked up to the fence. Mercy had given up on me long ago, but when she saw Charlie coming, she raised her head high and trotted right over to the fence. "Hello, darlin'," Charlie said. His voice sounded like rusty wire, but it felt friendly all the same. He scratched the horse around the ears and gave her neck a pat. He had some leather straps over his shoulder. He reached for them and then turned to me. "This here is the bridle. The silver bit goes in her mouth. This goes up over the ears like that, and you buckle it down here."

I didn't move. I watched and I paid attention, but I couldn't make a sound. I know now that it was grief that turned me to stone, but at the time I tried hard to move, to say something, to feel anything at all.

Charlie went down to the gate and led Mercy out of the pen and back near the saddle he had put down on the ground. A blanket was lying over the fence and he folded that in half and put it on Mercy's back. She stood real still. Then he put the saddle on and buckled up some straps. He kept talking to the horse. "Good girl. That's it. Move over." Stuff like that. After he was finished, he turned to me. "Sarah, you want to sit up on her back?"

"My name isn't Sarah anymore. It isn't Sarah Paul and it isn't Sugarplum."

"Fair enough. What would you like me to call you?"

"Sadie. I want to be called Sadie."

"Okay, Sadie. How about I make a cowgirl out of you. Do you want to try sitting up on the back of this beautiful horse?"

I was scared to death. I didn't want to be riding a horse or talking to this stranger or standing in the middle of this barnyard in South Dakota without a clue of what was coming next.

"I know you've never ridden before, and I don't want to scare you. I don't mean you need to go for a ride or nothing. Just sit up on top there, and see if you like the feel of it. I won't let the horse move. See. Mercy stands here real nice and quiet like. What do you think, Sadie?"

I stood up. Only friends called me Sadie, and the way things were looking, Charlie was as close to a friend as I had at the time. "I'll try."

"That's the spirit. You need to put your left foot up

here in the stirrup and then swing your right foot up over. I'll give you a hand."

I got up on the horse. The saddle was wide between my thighs. She was huge. I could feel every breath she took. In and out. In and out. Her neck twitched, and I jumped. "She's just getting rid of flies," Charlie said. His voice was calm. "How do you like the view up there?"

"Fine," I said. I looked around and tried to relax. I was twelve-and-a-half years old, and nothing I saw looked slightly familiar.

I sat there for a while looking around as the sun set on the farm. Charlie stroked Mercy's neck and spoke in that soft, comforting voice. "There, there. Good girl. Yeah. You stand up nice and pretty for this young lady. She's a special one. My niece. Can you believe it, Mercy? I finally get to meet my one and only niece, and Sadie finally gets to sit on top of a beautiful horse for the very first time. So you sit nice and let her enjoy the ride, because one of these days, if it's okay with her, we're going to let you start walking a bit so as she can see how nice it feels to be on such a smooth, graceful horse. I'll lead you around the yard as long as she wants, but not until she's ready. You stand there and look pretty, you hear?"

Charlie kept petting Mercy's neck and running his

hand down her front legs. He scratched her ears and let the reins go slack, but she didn't move. "I haven't had any time to talk to Sadie about any of this. The fact is that her mother needed some help, and I said I was happy to watch her daughter for a couple of weeks, but I don't know how Sadie must feel about it." Charlie glanced up over his shoulder at me. I pretended I was a statue in the middle of Boxer Park back home in Arkansas. A statue riding a statue of a horse. I sat up tall and looked out past the road to a cornfield that stretched out like summer itself in both directions. Charlie continued, "I haven't talked to her about it yet, but, easy girl, easy . . ." Mercy shifted legs back and forth. I rocked in the saddle, "but I bet when she is ready to talk we'll have us a nice conversation."

"My mother told you two weeks?"

"She said about that. Maybe a couple more."

"School starts in less than four. What if she ain't back? What then?"

"Sadie, I don't rightly know. I expect we need to take this one day at a time. Concentrate on the things we do know. I have an extra bedroom with a nice big bed in it for you. The sheets could probably use a washing; it ain't been slept in for a long time. And there is plenty of fun stuff for a girl to do around here for a couple of weeks, especially if you ain't spent any time on a farm. We'll be okay. Hey, Martha has a batch of kittens out in the barn. Want to see some kittens?"

"Sure." I relaxed my statue pose.

"Do you want to ride Mercy over there or get down and walk? I have to take her over and comb her anyway."

"I'm afraid."

Charlie looked up at me real serious. "That's okay. Mercy won't hurt you and neither will I. We're both real glad of the company. But there is plenty of time to ride this horse if you'd rather get down now."

"Yes, please."

Charlie lifted me off the horse with his strong right arm. "Whoa, Mercy. Good girl. Good girl."

Charlie handed me one of the reins and I took it. We both held on to Mercy and led her over into the barn.

Inside it smelled like dust and straw and manure, but it wasn't a real strong smell. Not that bad at all. Charlie took Mercy into one of the stalls and tied her up.

"Over here," he motioned toward another stall that was empty. In the front was a place to feed the horse. It was full of straw. A big old gray and white cat curled in the middle and six busy kittens crawled all over her. One was pure white, two were black and white, two were black and gray and one was a pure gray.

"Smoke," I said.

"What?"

"That gray one. That one should be called Smoke."

"On this farm there's a rule that if you name a kitten, the kitten is yours to keep."

"Really? You mean it?" I looked right up at my uncle. I had never had a pet in my life. My mother didn't want the responsibility. Thinking of my mother took the smile from my face. "My mother would never let me keep it. She hates pets."

"You let me worry about your mother. She's my sister you know. I was handling her for years before you were even born. Smoke belongs to you, Sadie. She has to stay with her mother for another week or so, but you can play with her out here. Then she's all yours. Get to know the mother cat. Give her a little attention first. Then she'll be more than happy to have you playing with them babies. It will give her a little time to herself. I'm going to curry Mercy now."

So I stood there, leaning over the manger and got to know that family of cats while Charlie stood in the next stall and combed Mercy with a round metal comb until she shone. He lit up a cigarette, and the smell wafted over to me. It smelled at first like Wes' car. It smelled a bit like smoke and burning leaves and late fall. It smelled like a new, unfamiliar place on a farm in South Dakota. I picked up that kitten and held it in my cupped palms. I found myself talking to it in a slow, soothing voice, a voice meant to calm any fears. "There, there, that's it. It's all right, girl. Don't worry. It'll be okay."

2

When I was little my mother used to read to me before I went to sleep. There was this big book of fairytales with black-and-white drawings of all the scary characters who wanted to eat me up or bake me in an oven. I remember cuddling close to her on the pillow and looking carefully at the illustrations in case there were clues that I could use to save the poor children in distress.

Mother liked poetry too. Sometimes she read from her old high school literature textbook. There was this one poem about a little girl going out to sea with her father who was a fisherman. A storm came up, and he tied her to the mast so that she wouldn't fall off the boat. The storm got worse; the boat crashed into a reef. The little girl, still tied to the broken mast, was helpless to save herself when she was flung into the icy water. I remember that her long hair was frozen on the waves when they found her body the next morning.

It was such a sad poem, but I loved it. I begged my mother to read it to me. "Sometimes, Sugar Plum, you remind me of a dark river," she said, but she read it again and again. I was so young that I thought, maybe this time the little girl will make it. I tried to concentrate, as if thinking would send her the message that she needed to beg her father not to tie her up. I wanted the little girl to tell her father that she was strong enough to hold on all by herself. I wanted to tell her that she was strong enough, but I never said a word out loud. I was a dark river; I couldn't save anyone from drowning.

When I got older, Mother gave up reading to me at night. She said I was getting too old to be read to. Instead, she taught me how to play cards. We used to play Concentration on my bed before I went to sleep. I watched her hands carefully and tried to memorize the cards. I practiced during the day on my own, finding pair after pair, over and over again. I got good enough that sometimes I beat her. I watched her eyes when I found a match and over time, she grew less interested. She looked away when I remembered the location of a card. Then one night, she had been drinking and fighting with Dad, and when we started to play, she wasn't concentrating. I didn't know what to do. I let a couple go, hoping she would see my mistake, but she didn't. Finally, I just matched them up to get the game over with.

"Well, aren't you the smart one?" she said with a smile. "I guess it's not my day."

"I was just lucky, Mother," I said.

"Yeah, lucky you." She pushed the hair off her forehead, finished her drink, and walked out without saying goodnight. We didn't play Concentration again.

One night, months later, when Dad had been gone for a few days after some argument, she came in and wanted to know if I'd like to learn how to play Blackjack, but I knew she didn't really want to play. She was just going through the motions, wasting time. I said sure, and she taught me the rules. It was the only time we ever played that game.

3

That night, Charlie made eggs and fried potatoes for supper. "Would it be okay if you sleep on the sofa tonight, so I can get your room ready?" I nodded. "You can watch the late movie if you like. Do you like westerns? I think there might be a good western on NBC."

I fell asleep in the dim light of the television in the living room while some cowboys rode around in a black-and-white canyon with their guns drawn. Charlie was working in the kitchen. When I woke up the next morning, it was spotless; all the counters were empty and gleaming white. The floor was shiny. Even that ancient stove was polished and looked like new. I must have looked surprised when I walked in. Charlie was at the table with coffee and a cigarette. He chuckled. "Can't have a girl living in a bachelor's pigsty now can we? You ready for breakfast, Sadie?"

My eyebrows went up. "Yes, sir."

"Sir? How about that. Start cleaning like a Marine, and they start treating you like one." He shook his head and smiled. "Haven't been called sir for as long as I remember, except of course for those telephone operator ladies when I call to ask for the correct time. So, two eggs?"

"Over easy, please." I felt like I had been sleeping for weeks, and I was finally waking up.

Charlie had a way about him that fascinated me. He looked sort of rough and worn out on the outside, but had a smile that reached all the way across his face, and he never seemed to get tired out. After breakfast, he went out to feed and exercise the horses. He told me to take a walk around the farm and get to know the place.

I visited Martha the cat and her kittens. Smoke was all curled up asleep, and when I reached in to touch her, Martha could have cared less. I guess some mothers let go pretty easily. I sat in that barn for a long time, telling Smoke all about me and my little yellow house by the river that Mother had lost because she spent all of her paychecks on lottery tickets, pull tabs, and blackjack tables and didn't pay the rent. I told her about my two friends, and how I never got to say a proper good-bye because my mother decided two days before we were going to leave to pack everything up in boxes from the liquor store and leave town on a Sunday afternoon. I tried calling my friends to tell them good-bye, but no one ever answered the phone. I told Smoke how bad I felt about that, how alone I was, and how scared I was that my mother wasn't going to come back for me at all.

I walked out into the trees and picked wildflowers for the kitchen table. The grass was almost up to my knees and tickled my legs when I walked through it. When the wind blew through the trees, the grass moved around and made a crisp, rustling sound. It smelled like summer out there in that grove. It made me feel a lot better.

When I went back to the house, Charlie had his shirtsleeves rolled up and was washing something at the sink.

"Ever had pheasant?" he asked.

"No."

"Shot this one right outside that shelterbelt last fall. It's the last one in the freezer. Good thing the season opens up again soon. They are a mighty tasty bird, but you can judge for yourself in a couple of hours."

I sat down at the table to watch him. "You thirsty?" Charlie asked. I shrugged. "I got some orange juice and there's always nice cold water. Thought we'd go to town this afternoon and get groceries and maybe a can of paint. I looked at that bedroom you're going to be in, and

I reckon it could use a little brightening up. What do you say? Would you like to pick out a color to paint them dirty old walls?"

I looked down at the table. That knot started tightening up in my stomach again. I didn't know anyone who would paint a bedroom for a guest who was only staying two weeks. "Did my mother tell you she wasn't coming back?"

Charlie turned full around. "No, Sadie, she didn't say that at all. I just figured your mother may not be too good about being on time, and if a few weeks turn into four or five, I thought you might like a nice room to cheer you up. A place you could call your own. That's all."

I looked right at Charlie and didn't feel so sad anymore. "That would be nice." I knew as sure as the fingers on my hand my mother would not be driving in that driveway again before all the leaves were off the trees. I'd be starting school in a strange place and getting used to a new set of rules all over again.

What I didn't know was that she would never return at all. She and Wes would cozy up in some trailer park out in Las Vegas, and the first time she would call would be four days after Christmas. Wishing us both happy holidays and how was her little girl doin'? Telling me the job market was depressed, and it wasn't possible to send for me just yet. Telling Charlie she was sure he was a better influence on me than she had ever been, and she'd get me as soon as she could swing it. Telling us all that, and forgetting to give us her address or phone number before she hung up, before she told us to have a Happy New Year.

I didn't know that Charlie needed someone in his life to need him. Someone to accidentally remind him about all the joy and beauty out in the world. Someone he could build a snowman and a snow horse with. Someone he could cook filling and delicious hot meals for. I didn't know, but that someone was me.

I didn't know what was coming, but that afternoon, after a big meal of pheasant and baked potatoes and corn, we went into town and bought groceries and sky-blue paint for my new bedroom. We got two paintbrushes because Charlie said this was a partnership paint job, and a twelve-year-old girl was plenty big enough to help paint her own bedroom. We moved the furniture out of the room; I wore an old bandana around my head, and Charlie sang cowboy songs while we covered the dirty tan paint with a fresh sky. No one had ever asked me how I wanted my own room to look. No one had ever let me paint a part of the sky before. I was as happy as I could ever remember being.

. . .

When we finished the first coat, Charlie lit a cigarette and squinted at me through the smoke. "Time for a break," he said.

I smiled and stretched my arms up over my head. The bedroom looked fresh and clean. The tree outside the window was bursting with heavy green apples. A red pickup truck drove by, leaving a cloud of dust behind it.

We had a glass of cherry Kool-Aid in the shade on the front steps of the house. We sat real quiet and enjoyed the rest. My arms were tired from painting.

"You want to go out and visit Mercy?" Charlie asked. "I'd like to check the horses."

I felt peaceful and content. "Maybe I could sit on Mercy again."

"Fine idea," was all Charlie said. When we walked out toward the barn, Charlie took my hand. I looked up at the sky, and I will always remember how it looked that day. Pure blue, as far as I could see.

4

The next few days went by quickly. I got to know my way around the farm, and it seemed like Charlie cleaned everything in sight. I asked him if he always cleaned so much.

"If you take a look around at all the cobwebs and the piles of junk in this little house Sadie, you'd have a pretty good idea that I don't spend as much time on it as some, but let's say I'm doing my spring cleaning in the summer. A little behind this year, yes sir." Charlie laughed. He always talked out of the half of his mouth that didn't have a cigarette hanging out of it. "Yep, this Marine is working double time puttin' on the shine."

I told him it looked real good, and it did. After I had been at the farm a week, Charlie said Smoke was ready to leave her mom. We went up into the attic to see if there was an old basket she could have for a bed. The attic door was opposite the stairway going up to my room. It was a door about half the size of a regular one. A window at the end of the attic let in some light.

"Be careful where you step," Charlie said. "Only step on these wide boards. We don't want to end up going through the kitchen ceiling."

There wasn't much in the attic besides some boxes and a few beat-up trunks. In the corner was a pile of wooden bushel baskets and a couple of floor lamps.

"Hey, I bet this old brass lamp still works. Would you like a reading light in your room, Sadie? Are you a book reader?"

I smiled. "I guess. I don't have any books, but I might get one sometime."

Charlie coughed and laughed. "It seems like we could rustle up a book or two for you from somewhere. Let's haul this lamp down and give it a try."

I balanced on the wide boards and tried to get out of the way, so Charlie could take the lamp over by the door. He got a bushel basket for Smoke. "We'll put an old pillow in here. Your cat will have a bed fit for a queen," Charlie said. Then he pushed a small box aside. "Well, will you look at this: your mother's baby doll."

He picked up the box and I could see the doll through the cellophane window on the package. It said

"Crybaby" on the box. Charlie laughed so hard he coughed. "You want this old doll, Sadie? Your mom used to tip the doll over and it cried like a sick lamb. It drove me near out of the house until I wanted to smash the noisemaker right out of that thing. Matter of fact, I may have done it. She may not be a crier anymore."

I didn't know what to say. Having my mother brought into the conversation made her seem far away again. Like a burn on your finger that doesn't hurt if you can only keep your mind off of it. I shrugged my shoulders.

Charlie handed me the box. "Let's get out of here. The dust is getting to me."

I took the doll. She was silent and had a twist of blonde hair near her forehead and a off-white dress with aqua ribbon trim. Her eyes were blue. She looked like no one had ever played with her.

We crawled out of the attic and dusted off our clothes.

"I remember that doll crying at all hours of the day and night. Seems every time it was jostled it took to wailing. Look and see if there's any damage to the body where an older brother may have performed surgery."

The doll's back was caved in a bit, like maybe it had been hit.

"That's what I thought." Charlie smiled. "I seem to remember something about a hammer. I must have been a nasty little cuss. Dad probably tanned my britches for that one."

"She looks so perfect otherwise," was all I could think of to say.

"Yep. Perfectly quiet. Probably lost her charm once she didn't cry no more."

The reading lamp worked, and we found a pillow for Smoke's bed. I brought her up from the barn, and Charlie got a blue glass ashtray for her food and a metal bowl for water. We put it in the corner of the kitchen by the pantry.

Charlie filled the water dish and carried it over to the corner. He took slow, easy steps and set it down carefully, and for no reason at all, my eyes filled with tears. I brushed my cheek with the back of my hand, but Charlie had already straightened up and saw me. He didn't let on. "How about after I feed the horses we run over to Brookings and see about getting you a book or two?"

I nodded. My throat was full of happiness, longing, and confusion. My mother's doll sat up on the dresser in my room staring at me when I walked in. One week had gone by. No letters, no phone calls, no news. I walked over and stroked Smoke, asleep in her basket in the sun. The world was a confusing place. My heart felt like it was filling up with happiness and bleeding with pain all at the same time.

5

My mother used to love to make French toast. She had a real sweet tooth, and sometimes, in the middle of the afternoon, she would decide it was time for some French toast. Once when she was in a good mood, she told me to sit down, and she pretended we were in a restaurant. She put a pencil behind her ear, tied on an apron, and asked "May I take your order, Missy?"

"I would like some French toast, please," I said.

"And what would you like on that order?" She twirled her pencil and smiled down at me. She was so beautiful when she smiled.

"Chocolate chips?" I asked, figuring I would take advantage of the moment.

"Well now, there's an original order. I'll check with the kitchen and see if we can accommodate that young lady." She winked at me. I remember that Patsy Cline was singing "I Fall to Pieces" on the stereo. It was summer, and the breeze was blowing the curtains in onto the table. I sat up straight, listened to my mother sing along with Patsy, and watched her work in the kitchen.

We ate French toast with chocolate chips melted on top and smothered in maple syrup. Mother drank coffee, and I drank milk out of our best china cups.

I knew it was a time to be very careful. I will never forget how tiny and thin the handles were on those cups. There were little painted violets along the inside of the top of the cup, and when I went to take a sip, the china rim felt paper-thin. I ate until I was so full I thought I would burst.

6

August was a very busy time on a farm. Most days Charlie was up early and out in the fields before I even got out of bed. He cut alfalfa and baled the hay for the horses to eat over the long winter. He helped the neighbors from the next farm, and then they helped him get in his hay. I asked if there was anything I could do, and after thinking about it, Charlie said I could try driving the tractor if I wanted to.

That's how I met the Rasmussen twins. Kevin and Cal were fourteen years old that summer, but you would never know it. They were identical twins, almost as tall as Charlie and built like Paul Bunyan, as Charlie used to say. They had blond hair and blue eyes and were tan from working in the fields all summer. I never paid much attention to boys before that, but when they came into the yard riding on the back of a flatbed trailer, their long legs hanging over the side, I looked twice. I suppose identical twins get stared at a lot, but I was trying to figure out which one of them was cuter than the other one.

Charlie came out of the house with his thermos of coffee and a cooler full of food for us. Mr. Rasmussen drove the tractor that was hooked to the flatbed.

"Morning, crew," Charlie said. He tipped his cowboy hat back and looked up at the sky. "It's a fine day for baling hay." I followed him up to the tractor, looking down at the ground and his cowboy boots. "Eugene, this here is my niece, Sadie. She is going to have her first try at driving the tractor. Sadie, this is Eugene Rasmussen from down the road west of here, and these here are his two boys, Kevin and Cal."

I looked up. The first one wore a blue work shirt and leather gloves. He winked at me. "Hi. I'm Kevin, the better looking of the two." He smiled.

Cal looked up, shook his head and nodded, as if saying hello. He wore a long-sleeve red T-shirt with a picture of a can of Coke on it. I will always remember that, because that first day I tried to keep the two of them apart by what they were wearing. The next day, when they showed up in different clothes, I was flustered because I couldn't tell them apart. I found out soon enough though; all I had to do was wait a minute, and I'd know. Kevin would smile or say something funny. Cal hardly ever said a thing.

I climbed up on the flatbed and rode out into the field with them. When we got out there, Charlie gave me a tractor-driving lesson. "Keep her going right down the middle of the row. I'll put her in low so we have time to pick up all the bales. All you got to do is keep her going straight ahead. When we get to the end, I will jump up and show you how to turn this thing around. All right, Sunshine?" He had never called me "Sunshine" before. It made me feel confident. I nodded and crawled onto the huge padded seat. It was a small tractor, and I thought it looked easy enough. Before I knew it, I was driving down the row as they picked up bales and threw them onto the flatbed. Mr. Rasmussen piled them all up in a nice, neat stack.

The first time I took my mind off the hay and looked up at the field and the farm in the distance, the tractor started running into bales. "Whoa!" Charlie shouted from the side. I must have looked real worried, because he laughed and pointed down the row. "That way, Sadie," he shouted over the noise of the tractor. "Keep her headed that-a-way."

We ate our lunch under a big cottonwood tree at the end of the field. "Are you going to go to school here?" Kevin asked, his mouth full of baloney sandwich.

"I don't know," I said. "My mom might come and get me."

"And if she doesn't?"

"Then I guess so." I didn't like talking about the future. It made me nervous.

"What grade are you in?" Kevin took a bite out of an apple and wiped his mouth on his sleeve. Cal sat there quietly peeling an orange.

"Seventh."

"We start in sixteen days; you better register." Kevin turned to Charlie. "You better see this girl gets registered for school. We could use a cute girl on our bus, and if you're smart, I can always use help with my homework." He glanced at me.

I could feel my face getting hot. It was probably bright red. No boy had ever said I was cute, let alone out loud and to my face. I could hardly swallow my food.

Mr. Rasmussen looked over at Kevin and shook his head. He turned to Charlie. "This one," he pointed his coffee cup at Kevin, "I never saw such a shy boy. I don't know what we're going to do with him."

Cal smiled. "Send him away to military school." His voice was soft.

Kevin punched him playfully in the shoulder.

I smiled and relaxed a little. He thought I was cute. I had to think about that one for a while.

. . .

I got the hang of driving the tractor, and the rest of the afternoon went by quickly. We took a break up at the house, and I got a beat-up straw cowboy hat of Charlie's to keep the sun off me. I was already sunburned and feeling pretty warm. Out near the barn, a haystack grew bigger and bigger with neat rows of sweet-smelling alfalfa bales. By sunset, we were all tired.

I went to bed that night feeling like I had been a big help. My eyes were heavy and felt warm from the sunburn. The last thing I remember is smiling when I thought about those two boys. Neighbors, at least for the time being.

Fall

7

"You suppose we'd better go into town and check out the big brick schoolhouse?" Charlie had taken apart a fishing reel and was cleaning it at the kitchen table. It was a Wednesday morning. All the hay was in, and Charlie said we'd go down to the creek and see if the Northerns were biting.

I shrugged and looked down at my toast and coffee.

"Seems to me since your mother hasn't been real good about keeping us up to date on her plans, maybe it's about time we made some of our own." Charlie put down the reel and lit up a cigarette. He always smoked when he did his thinking. He squinted through the smoke and studied me awhile. I could feel his eyes on the top of my head. "You like school, Sadie?"

"I liked it at my old school." My voice wasn't as loud or as sure as I'd wanted it to be.

"I went all my years at the school in town. Give or take a couple of old bats for teachers, it was a pretty good time. I think I learned enough to get me through. Got right in to the Marine Corps from there." Charlie got up and poured himself a fresh cup of coffee. He faced the sink when he said, "Think maybe you want to give it a try? Nice kids around here. You could meet some more kids your own age."

I felt like I was going to throw up. Not because I didn't want to go to school, but because my mother was missing in action, and I wasn't used to it. I didn't know anything about making my own decisions. "Sure." My voice sounded better, a little more positive.

Charlie turned around. "Let's go up and talk to the people in the office. We'll still have plenty of time to check out the fish in Elbow Creek."

Charlie drove up in front of the square, brick schoolhouse and turned off the pickup. He took a deep breath and brushed off the sleeve of his shirt. "Let's go, Sadie. See if we can get in and out of the principal's office without too much damage." He winked at me. "It's been a lot of years since I been in this place."

The office was small and smelled like floor wax and fresh paint. A man in an inner office stepped out and smiled. "Good day. I'm Clarence Ladner. What can I do for you?" The principal was very tall and what hair he did have was pure white. He shook hands with Charlie and then with me.

"Howdy. I'm Charlie, and this here is Sadie. She wants to go to the seventh grade."

He told us to come in and have a seat across from his desk. He got out a bunch of forms and papers for Charlie to fill out and started filling out some himself.

"What is your full name, Sadie?"

"Sarah Paul Sadler." I expected him to look up at that one, but he kept on writing. "You want to be called Sadie?"

"Yes, sir."

"Charlie, are you the father?"

Charlie looked up from the pile of papers. "Sir?"

"And you are Sadie's father?"

"No, sir. I'm her uncle."

"Legal guardian, then?"

"Nope." Charlie shifted in his seat. "Sadie is living with me for the time being."

"What is the status of her legal guardians?"

"Well sir, I don't rightly know. I'm taking care of Sadie until her mother gets back."

"Will this be a temporary arrangement then?" Mr. Ladner smiled and put down his pen.

"I don't know that, either." Charlie shifted in his chair again and then looked at me. "Sadie, why don't you go out and roll down the windows of our pickup so it ain't so hot when we get done here. Would you do that? Then come on back in. This won't take much longer."

I wanted to leave more than anything and was thankful once again to Charlie for bailing me out. I did not want to hear about how my mother was such a low-down kind of person that she drove off and left me without so much as one tear coming down on her cheek and mixing in with all her make-up, messing up her pretty face. I didn't want to think about her at all, because when I did, I felt such a loneliness and sorrow inside of me that I thought I might cave in or explode from the pressure of it.

When I got back, both men looked up and quit talking. "Let's show you your new classroom, Sadie," Mr. Ladner said. "Then I'll give you a quick tour of our school. Everything is looking bright and polished, ready for you kids next week."

So I was enrolled in the seventh grade at Aurora Consolidated School District #304. School started the following Monday.

Sunday, I washed out the only skirt I had in the bathroom sink. The washer in the porch had been leaking so Charlie did the laundry in town. I didn't have many clothes and couldn't make them last the week. I hung the skirt out on the clothesline and hoped it wouldn't rain. I took a bath and went to bed early. The bus was supposed to be at the end of the driveway at 7:20 sharp. My stomach was full of butterflies and worries, flapping around and making a terrible commotion.

I heard Charlie's truck start up and head down the gravel driveway just as I was falling asleep. I dreamed that he took off for Florida that night and decided to move where there were palm trees and leave me and Smoke and Mercy to take care of the farm by ourselves. I dreamed that I knew he was never coming back, but the next morning he called upstairs at 6:30. "Time to get up, Sunshine! Time for you to get some book learnin' again."

I could smell the coffee and the bacon. I rolled out of bed and looked around me. Smoke was sleeping, curled up in her basket. Crybaby sat on the dresser staring blankly ahead. "First day of school, Crybaby. Wish me luck." I turned and added, "If you happen to talk to my mother, tell her I'll never forgive her for this."

I went downstairs and had my breakfast. The kitchen was clean, and Charlie had packed me a lunch in a brown paper bag and written my name on it. "Sadie Sadler" in blue ballpoint pen. The bus came at 7:20, and I was on it.

. . .

That day, when I told Charlie I liked school, it was only a half-lie. I liked school until the fourth grade when I had Mrs. Henderson, the queen of mean. She had the reddest hair I had ever seen and talked most of the time with her hands in fists at her waist and her teeth clenched. "Sarah Paul Sadler if you don't stop looking out that window I am going to move you right up here to the front of the room. Sarah Paul Sadler what is the answer to number fifteen? You better figure it one more time." She was the only person who got away with calling me Sarah Paul at school. I told her every day that first week that I didn't like to be called Sarah Paul, that Sarah was fine thank you, but she never once left it off. When she had a headache, she would almost snicker when she said my middle name.

One time, when I was at her desk getting my math problems checked over again, she said "Why is it you have a boy's name for your middle name anyway, Sarah Paul?"

"Don't know, ma'am," I lied. It wasn't none of her business.

After conferences, my mother had said that Redhead Henderson was wound way too tight and didn't know how to relax.

So when I walked into that first day of seventh grade, I was almost expecting to see Mrs. Redhead Henderson standing in the front of the room with her hair all piled up on top of her head and her pantyhose sagging around her skinny ankles. Instead, Ms. Jamison stood in front of her desk with a smile on her face and a bouquet of daisies in her hand. She wore a long jean skirt and soft brown leather boots and had a thick black braid that reached all the way to her waist. "Good morning," she said, looking straight at me. She handed me one of the flowers. "Find a seat."

The other kids were sitting down holding daisies too. I couldn't believe I'd gotten a hippie for a teacher. I had never even seen a real one before! Ms. Jamison told us that her name was Ellen, and that was what we could call her. She said she was twenty-four years old, and this was her third year of teaching. She told us to look carefully at our daisies. "You can see our English studies right there in the middle of these beautiful petals. Poetry begins at the center of a simple daisy, as does science, mathematics, and social studies. All of it begins right here with the flowers in our hands. I want you to remember that learning starts at your fingertips and works its way all through your body and your brain and then, only then, can you give what you've learned back to the world."

Honestly. That is what she said, and then she smiled and started handing out our textbooks. By the end of class, there were daisy petals on the floor and green stems tossed around from desk to desk. I took my daisy, and with the top of my desk open so that no one else could see me, I put it inside the back cover of my math book, so I could press it and keep it nice. It seemed like a very important flower to me.

After lunch, we were in line to go to the library. I was the only new student in the class, and everyone knew everyone else. There were only two classrooms of seventh graders. Some kids said "hello" to me early in the day, but I ate my lunch alone and tried to get through the day as quickly as I could. It seemed to me that if I got the first day out of the way, things were bound to get easier.

"Careful in the library," a girl with curly red hair who was standing in front of me in line turned around and whispered, "the librarian is a real b-i-t-c-h." She smiled. She had braces on her front teeth and more freckles than I had ever seen. "I'm Karen Elizabeth McKinney, but you can call me Liza if you want. My friends do."

I smiled. "I'm Sarah, but my friends call me Sadie." I couldn't believe I'd said that. I had never even seen her before. Why did I think she would want to be considered one of my friends? I had only had two friends in my whole life, and then, well, Kevin Rasmussen said I was cute, but that didn't really make us friends. He did say "hi" on the bus that morning, but I didn't know if that meant anything. Anyway, I said it. Then I shrugged my shoulders.

"Sadie. That's a good name. I'll call you Sadie It sounds like a cowgirl's name. Are you a cowgirl?"

"Nope."

"Where do you live?"

"I'm staying outside town at my uncle's farm."

"Staying?"

"I don't know how long I'll be here yet."

"Oh well, you have to stay. We need some new kids in this school. Same old faces, same old stuff. It's boring, but you and I could change all that." Liza raised her eyebrows and smiled. The line started moving forward. "Talk to you later. Remember about the librarian, and be sure to put the books back on the shelves right where you took them out. She is real picky about that."

It was a small library, but it was full of books I'd never read. I checked out two and sat down at a table. I studied the other kids, memorizing their faces, their hair, and what they were wearing, figuring out how to fit in.

8

When I was seven, we lived in an apartment above a restaurant. Early in the morning it smelled like caramel rolls when they were baking them downstairs. Mother used to cuss "This is just damn torture to smell those rolls every single morning when we're stuck up here in this hot apartment eating Cheerios!"

Sometimes, if my dad had already left for work, and she was in a good mood, Mother would go down and buy a big warm sticky roll for us to share. "Now, don't tell your dad. He thinks he's the only one making money around here. Besides, girls deserve a treat." She licked her lips and always pushed the biggest half over to me.

On mornings like that, Mother usually put a record on the record player and danced barefoot in the kitchen. She sang along, and I loved to watch her and listen to her sing. She had a good voice and closed her eyes when she sang. I watched her swirl around the kitchen in her white t-shirt and shorts. I hated going to school on those days. I tried to memorize the feeling for later, when I might need it.

I don't know if Mother and Dad ever loved each other, but if they did, they forgot all about it when they fought. Mother told me that they started dating in high school because he was good at dissecting frogs and she was good at everything else. They were lab partners in biology; he touched the frogs and she wrote up the reports. Mother was a good student, but she said she never took much interest in it. It was easy, but it was boring. She never went to college, because, well, because I came along. That's what she said, "Then you came along, and well, that was that."

9

The next month flew by. Charlie was busy on the farm, and I was getting used to the new school. Ms. Jamison had us writing in our notebooks every day and reading poetry. I wrote in my notebook every night before I went to bed. Pages and pages of things I was thinking about. I even wrote a few poems of my own. Ms. Jamison said I was a poet. She wrote that, right in the margin next to one of my poems about Mercy.

"Yesterday, I got the mail on my way in from the bus," I said as I opened my milk carton and swapped sandwiches with Liza. She hated cold beef and I was tired of peanut butter. "There was something from the courthouse in Brookings. He read that letter over and got out a big bottle of whiskey from the cupboard on top of the refrigerator and kept drinking that stuff with his coffee until I went to bed."

"My dad lives in Brookings," Liza said. "He runs a dry cleaners there. What was the letter about?"

"I don't know, but I could tell we weren't going to be talking about it. Sometimes Charlie needs to have things quiet. I'm thinking it has to do with my mother." Liza and I had been friends for four weeks and two days, since that very first day of school. We did a lot of our talking at lunchtime.

"When is your mother coming back?"

"I don't know. She hasn't even called up once since that day she left me here. I hope nothing bad has happened to her."

"Maybe she got kidnapped or something." Liza's eyes were wide.

I stared straight in Liza's face. "What kind of a dumb thing is that to say?" I don't know where my anger came from, but it bubbled out. "How would you like it if someone said that about your mom?"

Liza looked down at her fingernails. "Sorry Sadie, I didn't mean anything. It's just two months is a long time. Why doesn't she call?"

I shrugged, sorry I had lost my temper. "I can't figure

it. Maybe she lost the number, or maybe she doesn't have a phone yet. It's expensive to call long distance. I bet she'll call me any day now."

When I got home from school, Charlie was exercising the horses. He didn't come in until almost dark. I warmed up some chicken noodle soup from a can and made us grilled cheese sandwiches. Charlie was real quiet, smoking one cigarette after another. We ate supper without talking at all.

Charlie got himself a cup of coffee. I hoped he wouldn't start putting whiskey in it again, because then he didn't talk at all. He went over to the whiskey bottle, but instead of opening the cap, he twisted it tighter and put it back up in the cupboard. "You like it here, Sadie?"

My throat tightened up. That familiar feeling of panic started in my arms and worked its way down into the pit of my stomach. "Charlie?" I said. My eyes were filling up.

"Sunshine, I'm only asking if you like it here." There was a pause. "You and me are doing okay, aren't we?"

"Yes, sir," I said.

"Since your mother hasn't bothered . . . since she hasn't contacted us yet to let us know her plans . . . the school and the county are checking to make sure you're okay. Some legal things. We need to go over and talk to a judge. If you'd rather . . . I mean you could live with a real family while you are waiting for your mother . . . if that's what you want." Charlie's hand shook as he reached for his coffee cup. "The judge wants to know what you want. We got to go over there on Thursday so you can tell him."

I knew I had to say something, lump or no lump in my throat. "I . . . want . . . to stay here with you," I said. I wiped tears off my cheek with the back of my fist.

"All right then," Charlie said. He put his hand over top of mine and patted it twice. "Then that's what you can tell him." He got up and left the room.

I cleaned up the dishes and fed Smoke my leftover soup. I took an apple out to the barn and gave it to Mercy. She stretched her neck out over the manger and whinnied when she saw me. She was real used to me by then. I hadn't ridden her by myself, but Charlie had walked me around the yard many times, and I fed her apples or carrots every day. There were three apple trees bunched together like best friends just out behind the house; Mercy seemed to like those apples better than almost anything. I got out the currycomb and combed her neck and back. I could see my reflection in her big dark eyes. I smiled at myself, surprised to see my image inside that beautiful horse.

Charlie came around the corner. I could tell by the way he walked everything was okay again. "Mercy, darling, are you getting enough attention from this niece of mine?"

"Could I try riding her, Charlie? By myself?" I suddenly felt an urgency to get past my fear.

"Right now? In the dark?"

"Please?"

"I guess so. Let me turn on the yard light, then we'll get her saddled up." I knew how to put on the saddle; I had been watching carefully. Charlie let me do it and then helped me tighten up the cinch.

I put my foot in the stirrup. That old familiar panic wasn't there in my stomach. Charlie wanted me around. He didn't have to take care of me, even if my mother never showed up. He said I could go live with a real family. I didn't know exactly what that meant, but when I swung my leg up over that tall horse and sat there looking around the yard at the house all lit up with yellow windows and the stars above it filling the sky, I felt good.

"Can I take her down the driveway and back?" I smiled down at Charlie.

He tipped his hat back. "Hold the reigns gentle. She's got a real light touch. She'll do what you tell her to."

I walked Mercy out around the apple trees, past the lilacs at the end of the house and down to the end of the driveway. The mailbox stood empty in the moonlight, reminding me again of the letters I wasn't receiving. Mercy and I turned around and headed back toward the barn. Her gentle gait was like a rocking chair or a boat on the water. There was no fear hiding anywhere inside my body.

10

The judge told us I could stay with Charlie as long as I wanted to, or until my mother showed up, if we kept in touch with the court and let them know if anything changed. The next Thursday, I rode home from school with Kevin and Cal and their mother. Faye Rasmussen taught high school English and usually stayed at school later, so the boys took the bus home, but she had to be back at the school for conferences after supper, so she left early. She saw me walking to the bus and asked if I would like a ride.

When I got to her car, Kevin and Cal were already in it, one in the front seat and one in the back. I could feel myself starting to blush as I got in the back seat, wondering which neighbor I was sitting next to. One had on a football jersey and the other wore a jean jacket. The one in the front turned and smiled. "Hey, neighbor.

How come you're sitting back there by him? There's room up here," Kevin said from the front seat. Mrs. Rasmussen closed her door.

"Oh, leave the girl alone, Kevin." She looked in the rear view mirror at me. "Ignore him if he bothers you, Sadie." She smiled at me and then at each one of her boys. "So how was school today?"

The boys both groaned. "Fine, Mother," they said in unison, "and how was your day?"

I laughed. Cal turned to me and smiled. "How do you like C. S. Lewis?"

"Who?"

"Your book."

It was on top of my stack of homework. "Oh, that. We just started it for class."

"If you like it, I have the whole series. You could borrow them. They're cool."

"Thanks." I looked out my window, trying to think of something else to say.

"Is Charlie going to your conference tonight?" Mrs. Rasmussen asked me.

"I think so," I said.

"How do you like Ms. Jamison?"

"I like her. I've never had a teacher like her before."

Kevin turned around. "I had her last year. She gave too much homework, but she was okay, for a teacher I mean." He punched his mom playfully in the arm.

Mrs. Rasmussen slapped his knee. "She does a good job. She has lots of energy. I hope Charlie can make it tonight. You try and make sure he does, okay?"

"Yes, ma'am," I said. "You can drop me at the end of the driveway. I get the mail."

"Come over sometime," Mrs. Rasmussen said. "I'll try to make sure these boys don't give you a hard time. In fact, we should have you and Charlie over for supper. Charlie and I went to high school together. I haven't sat down and talked with him for years. Maybe we can get together after the crops are all in."

"That would be nice."

I thanked her for the ride and waited for the car to drive away before I opened the mailbox. It was something I needed to do when I was alone. Each day I looked inside the dark metal mouth for a small stack of white envelopes and a newspaper. Then I went through the stack and glanced at each letter for my name, written in handwriting I recognized.

11

My dad started working construction during the summers when he was in high school, and then full-time after that. His football coach got him the job, so he could quit when it was time to start two-a-days at the end of the summer before the season started. He was a good football player, and people in town remembered that about him.

A few years after I was born, we moved further south so that he could work a longer season on road construction. We moved around a lot but always lived in small towns. Both my parents said cities were for people with no place else to go, so they got all crowded up into each other's business, and what kind of a way was that to live? Finally, we settled into the small house down by the river, and they were happy for awhile. Then Dad started staying out later and later and not coming home from work at all, and sometimes he was gone all weekend. Sometimes they went for weeks without talking much at all. We had a secondhand stereo that Mother played all day long everyday. Country and western music was her favorite and filled our house up with sound when there were no other sounds to be heard.

And then one day, he just wasn't there. I remember his letter jacket hanging in the front closet before he left for good. It had little gold footballs and basketballs on the front and he was real proud of that jacket. I knew he was really gone when I went to the closet, and it wasn't hanging there anymore.

12

On Halloween night, I stayed over at Liza's house so that we could go trick-or-treating in town. I had never slept over at a friend's house before. My stomach was a little upset, like before I get the flu.

Liza and her mom lived with her Grandpa Everett. He was the banker in town and had a long brick house right next to the city park. Liza had her own swing set with swings, a glider, a trapeze, and a huge slide. Her own playground, right next door to the park.

Her room had pale-pink wallpaper and a thick red carpet on the floor. There were stuffed animals everywhere. "If we go down past the post office, we should stop at old Mrs. Gleiser's house. She gives away full-sized candy bars and sometimes caramel apples." We were lying on our stomachs on the floor. Liza painted my fingernails dark red. I was going to be a gypsy. "Of course, normally we couldn't eat those apples, in case they might have razor blades in them or be filled with rat poison or something, but my grandpa has known Mrs. Gleiser for fifty years and she's practically like family." Liza had her red hair up in two braids with a hanger braided through them so they stuck straight up in the air just like Pippi Longstocking's. With all her freckles and her overalls and striped shirt, she looked perfect.

I wore my only skirt and a summer shirt that was getting a little too tight. I didn't look much like a gypsy, but it was the best I could do. Liza said she had some jewelry I could use, and we would fix me up. She was quite a bit taller than I was and said maybe some of her old things would fit me. Mrs. McKinney helped find a big full skirt for me to wear that went all the way to the floor and a shirt that came off my shoulders. She said it brought out the brown in my eyes, and I looked like a beautiful gypsy. I was discovering that people in South Dakota handed out lots of compliments, but I did kind of look like a gypsy.

On Main Street, we ran into some seventh-grade boys from our class. They gave us some big pieces of colored chalk to write on the sidewalks or steps of the houses where people turned off all their lights and pretended they weren't home. Liza wanted to write some four-letter words, but I said maybe the person inside had a headache and couldn't come to the door, and words like that would only make them feel worse the next day.

Liza rolled her eyes. "You are too nice to believe, Sadie Sadler. It's Halloween; we have to do something nasty!" So, we went door to door and collected candy in our bags and tried to think of the nasty deed we were going to do.

We stopped in Smith's drugstore to use the bathroom. They were staying open late on account of it being Halloween, and they were the only place in town that sold candy. Folks had to restock if they ran out. Aurora is a little town, but every kid in the county seemed to be in costume and on the streets.

I was coming out of the restroom in the back of the store when Liza came up with a smile on her face. She reached in her pocket and pulled out a thin white strap. "I have an idea," she said. "I got three bras from the necessities corner. There are still a couple left for you. We can hang them from the swing set at the park."

"I don't have any money, do you?" I asked.

"No." Liza shrugged her shoulders. "We'll just take them. It's easy."

She said it like she had done it lots of times before and didn't have to think twice about doing it again.

"Liza, you need to put those back right now before we get caught. I mean it!"

Liza rolled her eyes. "It's no big deal, Sadie. You don't have to, if you don't want. I'll just get these."

"No! I mean it, Liza. You need to put those back." Liza looked down the isle and then looked at the floor. "I don't feel so good," I said, and I didn't. "I think maybe I ate too much of this candy. I feel like I could throw up right now, right here."

Liza shrugged. "Okay, okay." She pulled the bras from her pockets and dropped them on the toothpaste shelf. "Let's go home then. It's almost nine o'clock, and we were supposed to be back around ten anyway."

They were turning off the outside lights as we walked out of the store. I think maybe Liza got the message that I wasn't very interested in breaking the law or getting into trouble of any kind. Maybe I was afraid of getting caught. Maybe I wanted things to go as smoothly as possible for as long as possible. Anyway, we went back to her house, and her mom made us popcorn. My stomach felt lots better. We watched the late movie with her mom and her grandpa and fell asleep in sleeping bags in front of the TV in the living room.

When I woke up the next morning, it took me a minute to remember where I was. The brick fireplace and fancy furniture made me feel like I was sleeping in a TV show or a furniture store showroom. Mrs. McKinney made us breakfast, and I started thinking about Charlie, wondering if he had missed me the night before. They took me home around noon. Mrs. McKinney handed me a shopping bag as she dropped me off. "I put your gypsy costume in there. The blouse and the skirt are too small for Liza, and I thought you might have some use for them. Oh, and there's a winter coat that Liza outgrew. You are smaller, and I thought you might want to wear it for everyday . . . if you would like. If not, you can get rid of it."

"Thank you," I said. "And thank you for having me over."

Mrs. McKinney smiled. "It was our pleasure. Nice to meet you, Sadie. You'll have to come and see us again soon."

Charlie walked out of the barn as the car drove out of the driveway. I ran out to him with my bag of candy and my new clothes.

"Hi, sweetheart. How was your party?"

"Great. And I got lots of candy to share with you!"

"Let's go inside and take a look," Charlie said. "It's getting a bit nippy out here."

In the kitchen, I pulled the clothes out of the bag and tried on the coat. It was a warm, lavender jacket with a black fur-trimmed collar. It looked brand new.

"Where did this come from?" Charlie asked.

"Mrs. McKinney. Liza outgrew it."

I tried it on. I was so excited. It was a soft wool and the inside felt like satin. I smiled. Charlie studied me. "It looks real nice. I guess winter is getting close. You are probably going to need some warmer clothes and boots, huh?"

I had never said anything about clothes. Charlie had gotten the washer fixed, so I made sure I had something clean to wear to school, but my only pair of jeans was too short and wearing thin and I only had three pair of socks. "I guess I could use a few things," I said, "but there's no hurry."

Charlie reached over and ruffled my hair. "For a growed-up man, I can be awful stupid sometimes. You go get yourself some lunch. You and I are going shopping."

Winter

13

Long before Thanksgiving, we had snowdrifts pushing up against the house, making the whole yard look like a giant birthday cake with too much white frosting. I never saw so much snow. White fields surrounded the farm for miles; gray sky reached out in every direction as far as I could see.

It was an early winter. "A mean one," Charlie said. "Winters can get mean around these parts. It's our job not to get mean back."

Right after Halloween, he stacked straw bales around the foundation of the house for extra insulation. He caulked around the windows that didn't fit so tight anymore. We drove over to Brookings and got a bunch of groceries: canned soups and tuna, crackers and dry milk, "in case we get a long spell where we're snowed in."

Charlie didn't talk much in the grocery store, but as

soon as we got back in the pickup he started right up, like he'd been thinking the whole time about things he was going to say to me, but didn't feel like saying them in front of the cashier or the woman in the coffee aisle buying her Folgers.

When we got back in the truck that day, he lit up a cigarette and turned on the country music radio station. "I got me a feeling this is going to be one bad winter," he said. "One year, when I was a kid, we was snowbound for twenty-eight days. Alice, your mother, was so stir-crazy she decided to walk the mile to the highway so that the bus could pick her up there. They only had main roads open, see. I figured they could come to my front door, or I wasn't going to get no book learning. Alice walked out to the highway a couple of days, mostly to see her boyfriend I figured, but then she gave it up again until the plow come through the next week. They tried to keep the road clear. They'd plow it open again and again, and those old prairie winds just closed her right back up. We had some twenty, thirty-foot drifts that year."

"The last time we had anything close, I was on leave from the service on a two-week furlough. The middle of the second week your Grandpa Simon and I got socked in for eight days. I didn't mind the extra time off, but we ran out of beer and smokes, and I was right ornery before than old plow reached our driveway." Charlie laughed his gruff, choppy laugh. "Yeah, old Pa figured I'd better go serve my country some more. He said I was worse than a bull in a pup tent when I didn't have my smokes."

He laughed again. "Your mother and I fought like cats and dogs when we'd been cooped up in the house too long. One time--" I turned and looked out my window. Charlie had figured out a long time ago I didn't need to be reminded of my mother. "Ah well, that's history," he said. He turned up the radio and started singing along with Loretta Lynn.

Mother seemed to have forgotten me without any trouble, but I spent every single day pushing that stone in my stomach from one spot to another. The heavy lump wouldn't allow me to be too happy and enjoy the life I was living. The lump reminded me that it could all change tomorrow.

Charlie went pheasant hunting that fall and put lots of birds in the freezer along with the fish he'd caught over the summer. We went to the thrift shop in Brookings and bought a stack of books for ten cents apiece that would last me all winter. I was becoming quite a reader.

Ms. Jamison had me writing in a notebook, reading novels and poetry, and finding my own voice. That's what she called it. I looked for my voice every day, writing page after page of questions I wanted to ask my mother, poems I had written about my new life, fears and good dreams, plots from movies that made me cry.

My report card was better than it had ever been, and I was proud of myself for the first time in my life.

Charlie said my good grades deserved a celebration, and that I could have one of my friends over if I wanted. That Friday night, Liza slept over at our house. Charlie made frozen pizzas, and we drank Coke and watched Alfred Hitchcock's *The Birds* on NBC. Liza and I squealed at the real scary parts, which made Charlie laugh, and I closed my eyes tight, but Liza looked the entire time. She didn't seem to scare too easily.

Later on, we sat up on my bed painting our toenails. She had brought along fuchsia nail polish and showed me how to put cotton between my toes so I didn't get it all over. I thought it was silly, but I didn't want to hurt her feelings, so I gave it a try. Liza said that painting your nails was a good thing to do at a slumber party. That was when I realized I was having my first slumber party. I figured Charlie would laugh me out of the kitchen in the morning at breakfast when he saw my toenails, but I knew I could handle it.

"Where did you get that old doll?" Liza said. She blew a bubble and then grabbed the pink Bazooka bubble gum with her fingers and stretched it until it deflated.

"It was my mom's. Charlie and I found it in the attic."

"It looks awful old."

I nodded. "I don't play with it. It just sits there and keeps an eye on things."

"I bet you miss your mom. I miss my dad and he lives fifteen miles away." Liza finished painting her nails and waved her hands around in the air to dry the polish.

"Sometimes, but mostly I just want to slap her face or shake her real hard for what she did to me."

Liza's face got white. "Don't say that, Sadie. You can't talk bad against your mom. God doesn't allow us to talk bad against our parents."

I laughed. I'd never seen Liza look even the least bit scared before, even during the movie when the birds were pecking people's eyes out, and here she was pale and wide-eyed talking about God. "You believe in God?" I asked.

"Of course I do. I'm a Catholic. Don't tell me you don't believe?"

I shrugged. "I don't think I do. I guess I've never given it much thought."

"Well don't tell my mom that," Liza said. "I don't know if she'd let me hang around with someone who didn't believe in God."

"Liza McKinney you are full of surprises." I touched my toenails, and since they were dry, I pulled the cotton out from between each toe. "What do you think your mother would do if she found out I wasn't sure about God?"

"She'd invite you to our church and give you religious gifts on your birthday and Christmas and try to help you see the way." Liza licked her fingernails to see if they were dry. "No doubt she'd try to make a Catholic out of you."

"Well, then let's not bring up the subject of religion with her, okay?

Liza lay down on the bed and stretched her legs up in the air. She held her hips up with her hands and started peddling an imaginary bicycle. "Do you think your mother will come back for you soon?"

I didn't answer her. I sunk my head into the other pillow and looked down at the strange dark pink of my toenails. Smoke jumped up on the bed, curled up on my stomach, and started to purr.

"I bet you want her to, but I'd sure miss you if she took you away from here."

I didn't say anything for awhile, but when I did my voice was quiet and slow and what I said surprised even me. "Sometimes I don't want her to come back. Charlie's more of a family than she ever bothered to be. She was more interested in a blackjack table than a kitchen table, but if she could settle down, maybe she would like it back here with us. She could live here too."

I knew I wasn't talking sense, but I didn't have to. Nothing I said or did was going to make any difference in what my mother decided to do with her life.

14

One winter, when I was nine and we lived down by the river, we got a couple of inches of snow. My dad wasn't working at the time, and he and my mother and I got all bundled up and went outside to play. They made this big circle with two lines intersecting in the middle and taught me how to play fox and goose.

I was running as fast as I could, slipping and sliding and falling down over and over. My mother screamed at the top of her lungs when my dad caught her, and they fell into the snow, laughing. She was wearing this red turtleneck sweater and a big old jean jacket, and my dad kissed her right out there in the yard. She looked so beautiful. He looked in her eyes, and then they kissed again, and I remember thinking that it was the most perfect morning ever.

Sometimes memories like that can be good, but sometimes they form another rock in the pit of my stomach, and I have to make room for them.

15

When Faye Rasmussen called and invited Charlie and me to their house for Thanksgiving dinner, I answered the phone. I turned to Charlie, who was in the kitchen making up a big pot of chili. "We can go, can't we Charlie?" He looked down at the onions he was chopping and then back at me. I knew his first reaction would be to say no; Charlie didn't seem too comfortable around other people, but I also knew how to ask so that the chances were better that he'd say yes. "Please, Charlie? It would be fun."

Charlie shook his head slowly from side to side, as if saying "no," then said, "Yeah, all right, if you really want to."

I smiled and took my hand off the receiver. "We'd sure like to come, Mrs. Rasmussen. What time?"

. . .

Charlie bought a twelve-pack of beer, and I made some banana bread to take over to the Rasmussen's place. Thanksgiving morning, Charlie put on some dress pants I had never seen and a cowboy shirt the color of a robin's egg. He had just gotten a haircut a couple of days before. "You look real nice, Charlie," I said. His shirt had white pearl snaps for buttons. He cleaned off his cowboy hat and sat it on the kitchen table with both hands, like it was made of glass.

"Even us old cowboys clean up pretty good when we work at it." He winked at me. I got the feeling he was looking forward to our visit too.

When we got there, Charlie and Mr. Rasmussen shook hands in the porch and talked about the snow. Mrs. Rasmussen was in the kitchen and smiled when we walked in. "Welcome! I'm glad you both could come."

Charlie handed the beer to Mr. Rasmussen, and I handed the warm banana bread wrapped in aluminum foil to Mrs. Rasmussen. The men went into the living room, and I sat down at the kitchen table. "The boys are out finishing the chores," she said. "They'll be in shortly. What have we here?"

"Banana bread."

"It's still warm. Did you make it?"

I nodded.

"How nice. Let's get out a plate and slice some for the table."

We talked awhile. She told me to call her Faye. The boys came in, stomping snow off their boots and brushing it off their legs, pushing each other around in the porch, all the time Kevin's loud voice over Cal's soft, quiet comebacks.

Charlie and Mr. Rasmussen sat in the living room like it was a doctor's waiting room. They made pleasant small talk, but Charlie sat up real straight and always had one hand on his knee. That made me know he was uncomfortable, because he never sat like that at home, and the only other places I'd seen him look like that was in the principal's office when he enrolled me for school and at the court house when he had to talk about guardianship papers so that I could stay with him.

The dinner was wonderful. I had never seen a table so full of food: mashed potatoes piled high in two bowls, boats of gravy, sweet potatoes with brown sugar and toasted marshmallows, scalloped corn, string beans with almonds, two kinds of biscuits, two of almost everything. There were lots of things I'd never even tasted before, and in the middle of it all, the biggest turkey I'd ever seen. Silver candlesticks and a bouquet of flowers stood at each end of the long table. The dishes were real china.

I had a cloth napkin and a fancy glass for my milk. There were three pies to choose from for dessert.

After dinner, Mr. Rasmussen and Charlie went back into the living room to watch football and have a few beers. The twins and Faye and I cleaned up the dishes and the kitchen. We played twenty questions, Kevin told stupid jokes, and the time went real fast.

Once we cleared off the table, Kevin went and got the Monopoly game. Mrs. Rasmussen said, "It's a family tradition. The boys and I play every Thanksgiving. You will join us, won't you?"

"Sure." I thought about the idea of having family traditions, about families in general.

"If you need to borrow money, Sadie, I'm your man," Kevin said. "Remember that." Kevin liked to talk big. Cal, on the other hand, quietly accumulated property and wealth and had hotels all over the place before the rest of us knew what hit us.

Cal looked at me apologetically when my money got low. "That will be five hundred dollars." I sat in the middle of his hotel row. I smiled at him, and he smiled back. I suddenly realized that now I could tell the difference between the twins. I only had to get to know them better first.

. . .

After the game, the boys went in to watch some football. "What do you want for Christmas, Sadie?" Faye asked. We were putting the game away. I looked up, surprised.

"I haven't really thought about it," I said. "I've been wondering how I was going to get something for Charlie." I picked up a stack of Monopoly money. "I wish this was real."

"Ah, I see your point," Faye said. "It's pretty hard to ask for money from Charlie for Charlie's present, huh?" I nodded. "Say, I have an idea." Faye lowered her voice. "I've been meaning to clean out a storage room in our basement for a couple of years now, but I never find the time. The boys are busy with sports and their own chores. How would you like to help me? You could earn some money for something for Charlie. I think we could get it done in one day if we stuck to it. What do you say?"

"You don't need to pay me anything, but I'd like to help if you want me to."

Faye shook her head. "I don't need to pay you, Sadie, but you'd be earning it. Otherwise, I would be taking advantage of you. I could use the help, and I would like the company. It's nice to have another female around this place. You think about it."

I didn't need to think long. "Anytime you want, Mrs. Rasmussen, I mean Faye. I'd be happy to help. It being Thanksgiving vacation and all, I have lots of time."

· · ·

Two days later, I walked over to the Rasmussen's place bright and early. It was cold and the snow crunched under my boots. The sky was clear blue. I could see the smoke from their chimney curling up over the trees in the shelterbelt around their farm. It was quiet, still, and beautiful.

Faye saw me walking up the driveway from the kitchen window and waved. Their dog, Whitman, barked and ran to greet me, wagging his tail so hard he looked like he might shake it off. Whitman was a long-haired, black mutt and had a winter coat so thick he looked like a bear.

After I played with Whitman for a couple of minutes, I went to the house. "Good morning!" Mrs. Rasmussen wore jeans and a flannel shirt. She looked pretty, even in an old pair of blue jeans. She was tall and thin. Her hair was soft reddish-brown and wavy. She wore it pulled back in a French braid or a bun when she taught school, but at home she wore it down around her shoulders. I was always surprised when I saw it that way, because she looked so much younger. Less serious.

"Good morning. Boy, it's cold out there today," I said. I could hardly feel my toes. "Where I came from in Arkansas, it never got cold like this. I remember one time we got a little bit of snow, and you would have thought the world was ending. People couldn't drive their cars without bumping into something. They canceled school for two days, and the roads looked like a demolition derby. It was crazy." Faye and I sat down in the warm kitchen, and she handed me a cup of cocoa. "Where are the boys? Aren't they up yet?"

"Eugene took them down to Sioux Falls to get some part for a tractor. They were going to do a little Christmas shopping, so we have the house to ourselves." Faye smiled. She ran her fingers through the hair at her temples. Her fingers were long and slim.

I don't know what turned on my mouth that day, but I couldn't stop talking. We went downstairs and started sorting through boxes of old clothes and books and dishes and junk of every sort: broken fishing poles, deflated basketballs, pictures the boys had drawn in kindergarten. I told Faye that my mother never kept much of anything because we moved around so much. When we finally rented our own house on the river, I hoped we wouldn't be moving anymore, but then my father left us, and my mother started gambling even more, and the rest was history.

"When I got out of the car at Charlie's, Wes told me to get all my stuff out from underneath the seat. He told me not to forget anything. That was when I knew they were planning to leave me behind. My mother never said a word before that."

Faye shook her head. She sat on a stack of cardboard boxes full of books. "I can't imagine it, Sadie. I really can't. I don't mean to judge your mother, I never really knew her in school, but I have to say, any parent who could leave a child like that . . . who could leave a daughter as sweet as you are. . . well, she couldn't have been thinking straight."

I shrugged. "Seems to me she's had plenty of time to clear her head, and I haven't heard from her yet."

I changed the subject then, not wanting to talk about it anymore, but it did feel good to let someone else know the whole story. I told Faye what my bedroom looked like, how the sun reflected off the river in the late afternoon, how I got my own meals and wrote my own permission slips for school field trips. I think my teachers knew all along. I think neighbors knew I was raising myself, but sometimes adults don't seem to look too hard at what is right in front of their faces.

We had leftover turkey sandwiches and pumpkin pie for lunch. We spent most of the afternoon cleaning up the basement. Faye gave me a stack of novels and poetry anthologies to read. She said she had more books than she could find shelf space for. Some of the books were old ones they no longer used from the school. "You read these and you'll have a big jump start on high school," she said, "but more importantly, they are great stories." She smiled. "If you ever want to talk about any of them, come on over. I love a good discussion about books."

I held one of the hardcover poetry books in my hands. I could hardly wait to read it, but we were cleaning, and I was making money to buy a present for Charlie.

By four o'clock, the basement room was neat and organized, and we had hauled box after box out to the trash pile. Before I went home, I had a small, white reading lamp, a pair of bibbed snow pants, a wooden brush and mirror set that had never been opened, bath crystals and two bottles of perfume. Faye said she got gifts from the students every Christmas and could not possibly use all the stuff she got. She had to give me a ride home in their pickup since I had acquired two full boxes of books too. She also gave me ten dollars for helping. I wanted to reach out and take her hand when she pulled up to our house. I wanted to tell her thanks for listening, thanks for the presents, thanks for the money. I wanted to, but I couldn't. I just looked over at her, and my eyes started to water.

"Sadie Sadler, you are a special young lady. Now don't be a stranger. You come and visit me soon, okay?" Faye reached out and touched my hand. "Thanks for all the help today."

I nodded and swallowed hard. "I had a real good time."

We both got out of the car and took boxes into the porch. Charlie was out by the barn and waved. It felt good to be welcomed home.

16

At the beginning of December, Charlie and I went to Brookings Christmas shopping. We agreed to meet up at Nick's Hamburger Shop at one o'clock. Charlie wanted to give me a little money, but I said I had my own. I'd been thinking about what to get him for weeks. I planned on a new saddle blanket, but when I got to the saddle shop at the end of Main Street, I had to change my plans. Nice blankets started at $13.00 and went up from there. Cowboy hats were too much, bridles, too much. My ten dollars started shrinking in my pocket.

I decided right there anything having to do with money was a problem.

"May I help you?" An older man with white hair and shiny black boots stood next to me.

"I don't know," I said, keeping my voice steady. "I

planned on getting a saddle blanket for my Uncle Charlie, but they cost too much." I looked down at the floor.

"Well now, how much are you thinking about spending?"

I had a ten-dollar bill. I wanted to get a little something for Smoke, and maybe something for the Rasmussens and Liza, but I decided right there I could make them some gifts. "Ten dollars," I said.

"And your uncle is a horse man, huh?"

I nodded.

"What's his name? Does he live around here?"

"Yes sir, his name is Charlie Hammond. We live over by Aurora."

"Why, sure, I know Charlie. He's in here all the time." The man snapped his fingers. "Say, he admired an exercise lead the last time I saw him in here. I'm sure he didn't buy it. You want to have a look?"

It was a nice leather lead for exercising a horse in a circle. "It's on sale for nine bucks," the man said. "And for an even ten, I'll throw in a bolo tie. A cowboy never can have too many bolo ties."

The ties were marked $3.95, so I figured I got a real good deal. I picked out a black leather one with a silver horseshoe on it. The man gift wrapped my presents and put them in a shopping bag. I had plenty of time to window shop before I met Charlie for lunch.

• • •

Charlie told me the hamburger shop had been on the corner of Main Street for over forty years. He used to eat there as a boy, and they still made the best hamburgers he ever had. I knew when he said he had eaten there as a boy that my mother sat on the stool next to him and ate her hamburger. I knew she drank chocolate milk out of a small glass bottle with a paper cap, just like Charlie. I was learning about the history she never talked about, learning about it without speaking her name, even now.

Christmas could not come soon enough. Charlie and I went out, bought a tree, and strung popcorn for it. I made double chocolate fudge candy for Liza and the Rasmussens. I wrapped the fudge in colorful foil, and Charlie helped me deliver the gifts. I found an old rubber ball in the junk drawer, poked a hole through both sides, and ran a cord through it for Smoke. I ran around the house with it bouncing along behind me, and she loved to chase it.

Christmas Eve, Charlie and I had oyster stew and crackers before we opened our gifts. There were two presents under the tree for me and two from me for Charlie. I was so excited I could hardly eat.

. . .

"You have to open the big one first," Charlie said. He reached to his shirt pocket for a cigarette. I could tell he was excited too.

"Okay, but then you open one from me," I said.

I took the big box and sat down on the sofa. Charlie was in his recliner. Patsy Cline sang Christmas songs on the stereo. I took a deep breath. "Thank you, Charlie." For some dumb reason I felt like crying again.

"Now, don't go thanking me until you got a good look at it. How do you even know if you'll like it?" Charlie lit his cigarette and smiled through the other side of his mouth.

I opened the box slowly, trying not to tear the paper much. It was a cowboy hat! A soft, tan cowboy hat. I sat there and stared at it in my lap. "Oh, Charlie, it's beautiful!"

"Well, don't just look at it girl, try it on." Charlie laughed and shook his head. He put his cigarette in the ashtray by his chair and forgot all about it.

I put the hat on; it fit perfectly. Charlie stood up and came over to me. "Here, you got to give it a little attitude. Slant it this way a bit. You want to look friendly, but in charge." He stepped back and looked at me. "Fits real nice. That will keep the sun out of your eyes."

I stood up and hugged Charlie. When I looked up at his face, the hat fell off the back of my head, and he caught it in his arms. "Thank you," I said. I realized I had never hugged Charlie before, and there was no one else in the world I wanted to hug more. "Thank you for everything, Charlie."

Charlie let the hat fall back onto the sofa, and he hugged me right back. "Merry Christmas, Sunshine," he said. He stepped back and looked away, swiping his hand across his face. "Well now, you got another one over there yet to go. Let's get to it."

He sat back down in the recliner and reached for a puff from his cigarette. His hand looked to be shaking a little.

"Your turn now," I said and handed him the package with the lead in it. He opened it right up. "That lead I've been eyeing! How in the heck did you know I wanted this?" He seemed genuinely surprised and pleased.

"Good guess," I said.

"Thank you, Sadie. It's wonderful. I'll put it to good use."

I had my cowboy hat back on by that time, tilted a little like he'd shown me. I picked up my second present. It was a small box, maybe a glove box or a little game. When I opened it, it was a cigarette carton, and my confused look made Charlie laugh. "Look inside; the present is inside," he said.

I opened the end, and a photograph fell out. It was a picture of me riding Mercy from last summer. I looked up, confused, trying to say the right thing. "It's a nice picture. Thank you, Charlie." I smiled.

"No, darlin'. The picture isn't the present. The horse is the present." Charlie nodded at the photo.

"Mercy?" I didn't understand.

"Mercy is yours. Merry Christmas. You now have your own horse."

"Mercy? Mercy is mine?" I couldn't make sense of it. And then, all of a sudden, like a warm wind blowing into the room, I understood. He was giving me Mercy for my very own! This time I could not help crying. It scared me and surprised me, to have all that emotion attached to a happy moment. I had never cried from being happy before, at least not any time I could remember. I kept shrugging my shoulders and looking at the picture.

Charlie came over and sat down next to me. He put his hand around my wrist. "It's okay, go ahead and cry. Mercy and me won't take it personal." He smiled. "But what I want to know is when do I get to get my second present?" We both laughed then.

He liked his tie too. I wanted to call Liza and tell her about Mercy, but I wanted to spend the evening enjoying the warmth of it all with Charlie. I had never been so happy in my life. We ate chocolate fudge and watched "It's a Wonderful Life" until nearly midnight, then we went out to the barn and gave each of the horses an apple. I told Mercy the news as she nuzzled up to my cheek.

Walking back to the house, I looked up at the bowl of stars in the clear night sky. I knew that I belonged on that farm, underneath those stars, and I looked forward to the new year with joy.

17

Three days after Christmas, we got the blizzard of the decade. The snow accumulated and was whipped around by a frenzied wind. We walked out to the barn to make sure things were secured and all the horses were well fed before the winds got too bad. Twenty-four hours into it, we had had thirty inches of snow and twenty-foot drifts in some places. Charlie's car was completely buried somewhere in the yard. Not even the antenna stuck out to give us a clue. One side of the barn had drifts up near the roof. Charlie said that would help keep the animals inside warm.

He wouldn't allow me to go out to do the chores with him. He took a long thin rope and tied it to the front step railing when he went out. He said it was easy to lose your bearings in a white out, but the rope would take care that. "If I lose my sense of direction, I can just follow this back to the house. I'll tie it right here on my belt. Now don't worry. I'll be back inside in twenty minutes." He was back in thirty, and I was scared out of my wits.

We were having coffee and doughnuts when the telephone rang. Charlie answered the phone. His cheeks and nose were still rosy red from being out in the frigid wind chills "Hello. What? Well, you don't say. I'll be damned." There was a long pause, and I got a sinking feeling in my stomach that something important was happening. "Sure, you can talk to her, but how about you talk to me a minute first. We ain't exactly had much conversation in the past few months now have we?"

It was my mother. Charlie held back his anger. He had one hand on his hip and then reached up to his pocket for that familiar pack of cigarettes. He cradled the phone with his shoulder while he lit one up. ". . . No, I didn't say that. I just been wondering where the hell you've been. It would have been nice of you to call Sadie up every now and then; let her know you still remembered her. . . . God Alice, what do you expect me to say? Yeah, fine. Talk to her, then we'll talk some more." Charlie looked over at me and motioned toward the phone with his cigarette. He took a long drag and blew it up toward the ceiling. "Come here, Sunshine," he said. "It's your momma."

I made my legs walk toward the phone; I made my

hand reach out for the receiver and put it to my ear. I tried, but I couldn't say anything. "Sarah? Sarah Paul, are you there?"

I sighed. "It's me Mother, Sadie."

"How are you honey? Merry Christmas! I wanted to wish you a Merry Christmas. I know it's a couple of days late, but I've been real busy with a new job, and the telephone lines were so busy on Christmas day. I tried calling. I did."

There was a pause. I tried to think of something to say. "Where are you, Mother? What are you doing?"

"I'm waitressing in a nice restaurant. I work the late night shift. Been on two weeks now. I haven't got much saved up, but it's a start. Wes is looking for some office work. He don't like what he's been doing. Too darn hot to work in the sun, he says. How are you doing?"

"Fine."

"Oh, you're mad at me aren't you Sarah Paul? Don't be mad at me. You don't know how hard it's been. I been trying and trying to get things together, but it takes time. Wes says --"

"Mother, I don't care what Wes says."

"Don't you sass me, Sarah Paul. I'm still your mother. Don't you be sassing me."

I felt like there was a spider web connecting me to my mother, to Alice. A frail delicate web that had begun to tear. Standing there holding that telephone, I imagined taking a scissors and cutting each connecting strand one by one. "I don't mean to sass you. I just don't care about Wes." My voice was without emotion. There was no feeling of the familiar stone in my stomach; I was calm. The line was quiet.

"Well then, I hope you had a good Christmas." Alice had regained her perky voice. "I'll send you something soon as I get my feet on the ground," she said. "Talk to you soon. Good-bye, Sugar Plum."

Good-bye Alice, I thought to myself. I handed the phone to Charlie, who stood right next to me like a bundle of barbed-wire energy. I knew the line was dead, but he didn't.

"Hello? Alice? Hello?"

"She hung up," I said. "She didn't say where she was, didn't give a number. Alice isn't coming back, Charlie." I said it, and it surprised me. It didn't hurt. I felt detached, like a stranger. "She doesn't care."

I looked over at Charlie and shrugged.

"I care," Charlie said after a pause. "Maybe I shouldn't say this, but your mother never should have left you like that, without keeping in touch, without telling you what was going on. She never should have done that. I don't know why she done what she did, but I want you to know that you'll always have a home here."

He looked straight at me, the tension fading from his face. "I would never turn my back on someone I loved."

I smiled and swallowed the lump in my throat. There was nothing more to add.

18

Two days went by before the winds began to let up. The old house sounded like it was struggling to stay standing. One night at supper, there was such a blast that the windows rattled and the boards moaned. Charlie looked up from his tuna and noodles and winked at me. "Not by the hair of my chinny chin chin!" he screamed at the ceiling. "Now get on out of here!"

I shook my head and smiled. Wasn't nobody more entertaining than Charlie.

The first morning after the wind died down, we bundled up and went out to see how the animals were doing. It was still fifteen degrees below zero. The cold grabbed at me the minute we stepped outside. My throat closed right up, like there wasn't enough oxygen to breathe. I started coughing. "Pull that scarf up over your mouth," Charlie shouted. "Breathe through the wool." That helped right away.

Mercy and the other horses were fine. All I wanted to do was be with my horse. My very own horse. I curried her coat and filled up her manger with grain and hay. The water wasn't running too good, Charlie figured the pipes were freezing, so we brought in buckets of snow and the horses went for it like it was ice cream. I guess they were pretty thirsty, but it looked awful cold to me.

After lunch, the Rasmussen boys walked over. They were getting cabin fever and wanted to know if Charlie and I'd like to play some cards. Charlie said no thanks, he had a book he wanted to start, but the three of us played "Thirteen" and "May I" all afternoon. When Kevin wasn't showing off, Cal didn't seem so quiet. We all knew each other pretty well by then and had a good time playing cards.

Cal looked up at the clock. "We better get back. I don't want to get Dad in a mood."

"Yeah, it's about time for chores, and Dad doesn't need any new excuse to chew us out."

I looked from one boy to the other. Cal shrugged. "He's been in a bad mood ever since the blizzard. We lost fifteen sheep out in the storm. Then the east end of the barn started to collapse under the snow. A couple of the cows don't look so good. I don't know. Maybe it's all that."

"Whatever," Kevin said. "I just know he'll tan our hides if we ain't there in time to do chores. They stood up and started putting on their warm clothes for the walk home. "If school can't start up on Monday, we'll have to do this again. Next time, we'll have to bet some money, and then beating the two of you would be even more fun."

"You only won one of the games, big shot," Cal said.

"Yeah, but it was the championship," Kevin said. He turned and winked at me, "See you, Sadie." He hollered into the living room, "Thanks, Charlie! See you later."

Kevin made me blush and feel all flustered when he did things like that, but Cal was the one I wanted to know better. I kept wondering what he was thinking, what he wasn't saying. I watched them walk part way down the long driveway and cut across the yard. They walked right over where the fence was buried beneath the snow. There were no visible ditches, no sign of the road. The landscape was a white, sculpted lake with waves created by the wind.

Weeks later, we heard stories of herds of cattle that were found a couple of miles from home, all frozen down in some ravine. Snow had drifted over the fences in so many places they could walk right out. Barns collapsed under the weight of several feet of snow on the roof. One place west of Brookings had to get the cattle off the roof of the barn. One cow had already fallen through a weak spot, and the rest of them were just trying to get out of the snow. The drifts were so high that they walked right up on top of the barn!

Our neighbors up the road had to dig their sheep out of snowdrifts two different times to keep them alive. The dumb animals didn't move when the drifts started forming around their legs. They stood there all bunched together trying to get warm. Their barn had collapsed three days earlier, and when the winds began again, the make-shift shelter the farmer had made to protect them wasn't enough. Digging sheep out of the snow. Farming was a hard business out on the plains.

Lucky for us, the drifts wrapped our barn in a warm blanket of snow that kept the horses and cats safe inside. Charlie had to dig the door out a couple of times so that we could get in, but all the animals were safe, and there was enough feed in the haymow to see them through.

19

Near the end of January, something terrible happened, and the winds and the newly-closed roads only made matters worse. It was a Tuesday. The winds started up again late Monday night. I lay in my bed listening to the whistling around my windows. Last fall Charlie had tacked heavy plastic up on the outside of the windows to keep the drafts out and help keep my room warmer. I had grown to like the sound of the wind rattling that plastic, while I snuggled under my electric blanket in my bed. I was toasty warm, except for my nose above the covers. Sometimes I pulled the blankets like a tent around my face and let the heat rise up to keep my whole face warm. My room didn't have any heat in it; the only heat to the upstairs was in an open grate at the top of the stairs. Sometimes, when I woke up in the morning, my glass of water was nearly frozen solid. On the coldest nights, I covered my head completely and slept like a rock. It was hard to get out of bed on those frigid mornings.

That Tuesday, I got up early to listen to the radio to see if school had been cancelled. Looking out the living room window, I could see the trees along our road, which meant the wind had died down, but the road looked drifted in. Roads closed up awful fast when there was so much snow to blow around, and the winds the night before had been strong.

The light was on in the bathroom when I got up, so I went into the kitchen to make Charlie a pot of coffee and get us some eggs. I called into him, "Charlie, you want your eggs scrambled or fried?" He didn't answer me. It was real quiet. "Charlie? You okay in there?" I went to his bedroom, to see if maybe he had left the bathroom light on and the door shut, but he wasn't in his bed.

I went back to the bathroom, knocked once on the door, and opened it. Charlie lay on the floor; his skin was a whitish-gray color. His eyes were closed. "Charlie! Charlie!" I screamed, as if screaming would wake him up. The next several minutes moved like ice in a jammed river. I felt cold and slow and unable to think. I touched his face, and it was warm. It looked like his chest was going up and down. I ran to the phone and dialed the operator.

I told the operator Charlie's name and gave directions from the highway to the location of the farm. I told her I thought he was breathing, but he wouldn't wake up. She asked me if I thought our road was open, and I said no. She asked if there was a nice flat place on the yard where they could land a helicopter. I started to cry then. I didn't know about helicopters, and I didn't know what to do.

"Listen carefully," she said. "Make sure your front door is unlocked. Then go to your uncle and wait next to him. If he feels a little cold, put a blanket over him. Make sure he is still breathing. Put your ear to his nose. If you don't hear breathing, you'll have to give him mouth to mouth resuscitation. Do you know how to do that?"

"No," I sobbed. "I don't, ma'am. I really don't." I paused. "I've seen it on TV though."

"Okay, listen. Lay the phone down, but don't hang it up. You go to your uncle, and if he stops breathing, you come back here and ask me what to do. I will be on the telephone the whole time, and we'll send somebody out to help you right away. It shouldn't be too long. Try to stay calm. Everything is going to be okay. Do you understand?"

I nodded. "Yes, I mean, yes, okay."

"So go and make sure the door is unlocked now, then cover up your uncle and make sure he keeps breathing. Don't hang up the phone, just lay it down. Go on, now."

I did what she told me, and sat next to Charlie for what seemed like a long time. I could hear his breathing, but it was weak and slow. The next thing I remember is hearing a snowmobile pull into the yard. A man in a black snowmobile suit brought in a big satchel and said hello, then asked me to go out in the living room and watch for the helicopter to arrive. He took some things out of the bag, and I left the room.

Later, I found out he was with the Rural Emergency Ambulance Service from Aurora. The helicopter came from Brookings and landed right out in the yard.

They had tubes going into Charlie and carried him out on a stretcher. They told me to call a relative or close friend and let them know what had happened. Charlie would be at the Brookings Hospital. I could call there in a couple of hours to see how things were going. They took my name and my telephone number.

At first, I didn't know who to call. No face, no name came to mind. There were no relatives. And friends? Who were our friends? Liza was in Nebraska visiting relatives. Finally, the Rasmussens entered my mind, and I felt immediately warmer and not quite as scared.

Faye answered the phone.

"Hi, Mrs. Rasmussen. They told me to call you."

"Sadie? Are you okay?"

There was a pause. "They told me to call you."

"Who told you to call me, honey? What's the matter?"

"Charlie. It's Charlie."

"Oh, God." Faye sighed. "I heard the helicopter. Was that for him, Sadie? What's wrong?"

"They took him to the hospital. Something is really wrong. They told me to call a relative, but I don't have any." I started to cry again. I couldn't explain that Charlie was my whole family, my mother and father and grandparents all rolled into one quiet, gruff person full of love and care and patience. I couldn't tell her that for once I had a home, and I belonged, and just when I started to believe it all, when things were really going well--

"Sadie, listen to me, honey. I will be there in ten minutes. I'll be right there, okay?"

"Okay," I said. I hung up the phone and stood looking at it, as if it was Faye herself, and I would feel better if I stayed close to her voice.

Faye drove one of their snowmobiles over and stopped the machine right by our front door. She was bundled in a snowmobile suit and had a full-knit face mask over her face. I watched her come in the front door; she looked like a bank robber for an instant, and then she pulled the mask from her face, and her reddish hair tumbled around her shoulders.

She ran over to me and hugged me to her; she had tears in her eyes. She was cold and smelled like fuel and exhaust. "What happened, Sadie? What happened to Charlie?"

"I don't know. He was on the floor when I woke up, and . . . and he wouldn't open his eyes."

She held me for a long time. "Sadie, I want you to go upstairs and pack a few clothes, say two days worth or so. I'll call the hospital and let them know you'll be at our house. They can call us there. Then I'll get Eugene to see how we can get you over to Brookings; he can find out what roads are open."

She looked around the room. My cat, Smoke, was curled up on the back of Charlie's recliner in the living room. "You can bring your cat, if you want. It's up to you. It might be a scary ride for it."

"I'll just feed her," I said. I looked around the room, and in a split second, envisioned cardboard boxes and empty places were my life had been. Moving out, moving on. I walked slowly up the stairs to my room. Memorizing the place where Crybaby sat on my dresser, the basket where Smoke slept, the photograph of me riding Mercy stuck into the edge of the mirror. I grabbed some clothes and shoved them into my pillowcase next to my pillow.

Then, I suddenly felt so guilty. I realized I was worrying about myself, instead of worrying about Charlie. It was nowhere near over. I took a deep breath and went back downstairs.

20

Charlie had a stroke. It was two days before I could get over to the hospital to see him. The roads were all blocked, and the wind chill was a dangerous forty-degrees below zero.

"More fried chicken, Sadie?" Faye passed the platter, still piled high with chicken. Kevin took a couple of legs and passed it on to me. Cal smiled from across the table. The whole family was very kind and tried to make me feel at home. Kevin was almost as quiet as Cal and didn't flirt with me or embarrass me once. Sitting at the supper table that second night, I thought to myself that this might be what it would be like to have two brothers. Mr. Rasmussen was always quiet, but he seemed more distant that usual. Faye did everything she could to keep my mind off Charlie and try to help the time pass faster. We made cookies to take to the hospital. We played double solitaire. We washed and folded clothes. She French braided my hair.

The boys took the snowmobiles over to our place and did the chores for us. They reported that everything was fine. Cal told me he curried and brushed Mercy, and she ate the two apples he had taken for her. I missed Charlie and Mercy and Smoke, and I missed the farm, but these people were like family too. I was learning that there were many kinds of families, and most of them didn't look like those on TV.

Finally, the winds stopped, the sun came out, and the temperatures rose enough so that I could get to Brookings. Mr. Rasmussen gave me a ride on the snowmobile to the Bender's farm two miles away. They lived on the highway, which was open again. We borrowed their pickup, and Mr. Rasmussen took me up to the hospital. He dropped me off at the front door and said he would be back in a couple of hours. He needed to pick up a few supplies for the farm.

I remember all the white when I walked into Charlie's room: white sheets, white walls, white floor. Charlie had on one of those white hospital gowns, but he had some color in his face again. There were tubes and bottles and beeping machines surrounding his bed. He was sleeping when I walked in, but he woke right up when I stood next to the bed. I put my hand on his arm. He looked down at it with a curious look. "Hello, Sunshine. How's my girl doing?"

I had so many questions; I didn't know where to start. I tried to smile, but I was fighting back the tears. "Are you okay, Charlie? Are you going to be okay?"

"Well, this old cowboy is a little broken-down, but I don't figure they got to shoot me yet." The look on my face must have told him I wasn't ready for jokes. "I'm okay, Sadie. A little beat up, that's all. My left arm doesn't seem to want to work no more, but the doc says that may come back."

I looked down where I was holding on to his wrist. His hand was limp on the covers. "Can you feel my hand?" I asked.

Charlie smiled. "I can feel it some." He looked in my face. "I bet this whole thing scared you to death. I'm sorry, Sunshine." He looked sorry, and then his face looked angry, and he looked away, toward the window.

"What do they do now, Charlie?"

"Give me some medicine to thin out my blood, I guess. I don't know after that."

The doctor came in later and introduced himself to me. "I've been hearing all about you from your Uncle Charlie," he said. "I'd say he was very lucky to have you around, young lady. You saved his life."

I hadn't thought about that. "I didn't really do anything," I said.

"Oh, yes you did. You kept your cool and called for help. You did exactly what you should have done," Doctor Feldman said. "If you hadn't been there, Charlie would have been in a lot of trouble." He said if I had any questions I could feel free to ask. I felt free, and I asked a lot of them.

He said that Charlie's heart was working a little harder than it was supposed to be, and that he needed to take some medicine that would help. Charlie would be in the hospital for a while and then would have some exercises to do at home. Charlie had to watch what he ate, and most importantly, he had to quit smoking. He looked at Charlie when he said that part.

"We'll see, Doc," Charlie said. "I'm an old dog, and that's one new trick I don't know if I can manage."

"If you don't want to have another, perhaps more debilitating, stroke you need to change your lifestyle. It's that simple. Next time you may not be this lucky."

Charlie looked at me and changed the subject. "So how's that pony of yours?"

I looked at Charlie and then at the doctor. The rules were not familiar. I didn't know if Charlie was refusing to get better, or if getting better wasn't a possibility. I wanted to ask Doctor Feldman if Charlie was going to die, but I was afraid of what he might say. I looked down at the floor.

"Your uncle is a stubborn man, Sadie, but he's a reasonable man. He knows what he needs to do. I think he'll be fine. Good as new, if he does his therapy on that arm like he's supposed to." Then the doctor left, Mr. Rasmussen came to get me, and I kissed Charlie good-bye.

I talked to him on the phone a couple of times a day. By the weekend, all the roads were open, and Mrs. Rasmussen drove me to the hospital for a visit. She stayed and talked with us for an hour or so, and left me to spend the afternoon. She picked me up at suppertime. Charlie was going to be released by the middle of the next week.

We drove home in the quiet cab of the pickup until we turned onto the gravel road a mile from their place. "Things are going to be okay Sadie. I talked to the doctor. Charlie was very lucky. You know, he was lucky you were there that morning, but it seems to me his best luck is having you around full-time." Faye smiled.

I nodded, not able to believe that things were really going to be okay. I felt that old stone in my stomach, rolling around, looking for a place to rest.

21

February was quiet. We only had two snow days all month, and Charlie mostly slept and watched TV while he was getting his strength back. Faye took me to town to get groceries, and I did most of the cooking and cleaning. We ate a lot of tuna and noodle hotdish and dried beef sandwiches.

Charlie didn't seem very interested in doing his arm exercises. He kept on smoking, but he tried to smoke only half of the cigarette and then put it out. There were ashtrays all over the house full of half-smoked cigarettes. He didn't seem to be smoking any less, just going through more packs in a day. He also walked around with a coffee cup in his good hand. Half coffee, half Jack Daniels whiskey. Some days he started drinking before noon.

The second time they called school off early, Liza rode home on the bus with me. We figured if we were going to get snowed in again we may as well be together. Everyone was getting tired of the days off. School was a lot better than looking at the same four walls day after day. Going outside wasn't always an option because of the cold windchill.

When we got home, it was one o'clock. Charlie was watching soap operas on the television. He had his coffee cup and a cigarette. I looked at him and felt ashamed; I didn't want Liza to know he was drinking. His bad arm was tucked down by his side, hidden from view. "Hi, Charlie," I said. "We're home."

I turned to Liza. "Let's make some popcorn and go up to my room. We can play cards or something."

"So what all is wrong with Charlie, anyway?" Liza shuffled the cards as we sat cross-legged on the bed. I had brought the space heater up from the bathroom and the room was unusually cozy and warm.

"He had a stroke, so now his left arm doesn't work."

One of the boys in my class had seen Charlie in town two days before. He asked me about Charlie's arm at lunch. He said that Charlie looked like a puppet and that somebody cut the string to that arm. All the kids at my table laughed, and I laughed too. I thought of Pinocchio trying to dance. I thought of Charlie trying to cut the twine from a bale of hay for the horses. Trying to do the chores with one arm. Trying to open a can of beer, a can of beans. He tucked the bad arm into the pocket of his coat and left it there.

"Won't it ever work?" Liza asked.

"I don't know," I said. "It's your turn to draw." I looked down at the cards. I felt a wound, deep inside, when I remembered laughing at Charlie, making fun of the most important person in my life. I felt so ashamed.

Later that night in bed, we played with flashlights, shining them on the ceiling, having races to the corners of the room, making patterns and drawing pictures.

"Do you like anybody?" Liza asked.

"Sort of," I said.

"One of the Rasmussen twins?"

"Cal," I said. "How did you know?"

"I see you get in line for the bus. I've seen you smile at one of them; I just didn't know which one it was."

"He's the quiet one. Don't you ever tell a soul Liza McKinney, or I'll never speak to you again."

"Cross my heart."

"You like anyone?" I asked.

"David Williams, but I think he likes that stinky old Karen Rogers. Little Miss Goody Two-Shoes."

"Karen Rogers has more clothes than a Barbie doll," I said, feeling a bit of envy for all her nice shoes and jeans and dresses, her three different winter coats, all the ribbons she wore in her hair, and her pierced ears.

"My grandfather says her daddy has the biggest farm in the county," Liza said. "I expect she gets most anything she wants."

"So do you!" I teased.

"Do not!" Liza shined the flashlight right in my eyes.

"Do too!" I laughed and pointed my light at her face.

"Do not, chicken legs."

"Do too, dog breath."

We went on like that for a while and laughed until our stomachs hurt. It was wonderful to have a best friend. I hadn't laughed like that for a long time. The sound of the television filtered up through the heat vent in the floor at the top of the stairs; occasional loud screams and the sound of gunfire mixed in with our laughter and the howling wind outside my window, but I slept better than I had in weeks, not worrying about a thing.

We didn't have school the next day, so Liza and I had the whole day to ourselves. We slept in and when we finally came downstairs, I heard Charlie cussing in the kitchen and banging some pots and pans around. It seemed like he swore more every day and got in a worse and worse mood. Liza looked at me, and I shrugged. We walked into the kitchen.

"Morning, Charlie," I said.

"Yep," he said, not turning around.

"Do you want some eggs?" I asked. "I'm fixing some for Liza and me."

"Nope, coffee will do me fine." He filled up his coffee cup and left the room. He went through the living room, and back to his bedroom and closed the door. I shook my head, the pleasant mood of the morning gone.

"My dad drinks too much," Liza said with a whisper. "That's why my mom divorced him. Mom says he started taking longer and longer lunches and not going back to work at all. I don't remember it. I was too little."

"Does he drink when you visit him?" I whispered.

"Not much, but after I go to bed I hear the ice cubes hit the glass. I expect he stays up late at night catching up, because he always sleeps in real late now."

"It worries me," I said. "The doctor said he had to watch what he ate. He never said nothing about drinking, but I bet this ain't good for him."

Liza shrugged. "Maybe you could talk to him."

I felt like if I did, he might turn against me all together and send me somewhere else to live. After all, it hadn't taken much the other day in the cafeteria for me to turn on him. I made fun of him along with the other kids, and I couldn't explain why. I started to feel the familiar dance on eggshells: watch what you say, watch what you do, no one out there is looking after you.

22

One day at school, Mrs. Rasmussen stopped me in the hall. "Hi, Sadie. How are things going at home? You doing okay with groceries? You need any help with anything?"

"We're fine. Thanks, Mrs. Rasmussen."

"It seems like I never see you smiling anymore. You sure things are okay? I'm worried about you."

"Maybe I'm just tired of winter," I said with a weak smile.

"Well, I can understand that. Give me a call if you need anything, okay?" I nodded. "Promise?"

"Yes, mam," I said. At school, she was Mrs. Rasmussen. On the farm, I called her Faye. But no matter what name I thought of to call her, I didn't know how to tell her that I was trying my best not to worry about Charlie every minute of every day.

Liza's mom had me over for dinner one Friday night before a high school basketball game. She kept asking questions about Charlie, until I wondered what exactly Liza had told her. Everybody was nosey, trying to get inside of me and find out how I was feeling. Even Liza took to asking if Charlie still drank too much and still smoked them cigarettes.

That Saturday I cleaned the house real good. I washed the clothes and was doing the dishes after supper when Charlie came into the kitchen for more coffee. He kept the whiskey bottle in the living room now, on the end table next to his chair. He hadn't said but two words all day. Most of the time he sat and watched the TV, soap operas or game shows like "To Tell the Truth" or whatever else was on. I got tired of listening to commercials.

I'd been planning what to say all day, but instead of my planned speech, I went over to the dish rack and got three coffee cups that I had just washed and put them on the table. Then I took the coffee pot as Charlie put it down, and went over and filled each cup up halfway.

"Here. I'll get you a head start on your next drink, so you don't have to come out here each time to get it. Half full, isn't that right?" I put the coffee pot down on the table and turned to glare at Charlie. My hands were shaking.

Charlie looked over at me and squinted his eyes, like when he was about to reach for a cigarette and light it. He reached for his shirt pocket with his good hand. "You want me to light your cigarette too?" I said. He pulled his hand back, put it on the counter behind him, and tilted his head a little, as if studying me, as if I was a stranger he was seeing for the first time.

"I take it you got something to say to me, Sadie, so why don't you just spit it out?"

I was so mad that the words didn't get caught in my throat like they usually did. "I don't know, Charlie, but it feels like I'm watching you die a little bit every day, and I can't stand it anymore. When my. . . when Alice started gambling so heavy, I watched it all. First the money out of her purse, then she broke my piggy bank and took my money, and then she hocked the TV and the stereo. She finally quit getting groceries altogether. Day by day she looked crazier, and I got hungrier and more worried.

"You ain't trying to get better. You ain't using that arm like the doctor told you, and you're smoking all the time." I paused and looked down at my feet. Charlie didn't say a thing. "You told me once I'd always have a home here. What good is it if you ain't here? I'm your family, Charlie. I want you to get better, like it used to be. You can't keep everybody locked out. I may be a kid, but I know this ain't good." My stomach filled back up with anxiety and fear. I ran into the bathroom and was sick. I stood over the toilet and heaved until all that was left inside of me was the fear. Charlie knocked on the door; I didn't answer, and he came in.

He turned on the water and got a clean washcloth. He walked over to me and tilted my face up. He washed the corners of my mouth and my chin with his good hand. Then he took my hand, and we walked into the living room and sat down on the sofa.

Tears were streaming down his face. "I didn't think I'd be any good at this parenting stuff, but I didn't think I'd make this big a mess of it."

I wanted to comfort him, to say it wasn't his fault, but my words had dried up with my anger. We were both quiet a long time.

"When I was in Vietnam, there were so many times I wanted to help friends of mine, but there was nothing I could do. I would hear them crying in pain or in fear, calling out for help. It was like my hands were tied. I couldn't heal the wounded; I couldn't light up the dark nights so that they'd know where it was safe to step and where it wasn't. It was a bloody nightmare, Sadie. Week after week, month after month.

"When I came back after Dad died, I decided I wouldn't try helping anyone anymore. I'd just mind my own business and raise my horses." Charlie smiled. "Then one summer day, a car drove up the driveway, and sunshine came into my life. I didn't know how lonely I'd been until you came along and sat across the table from me at suppertime.

"It seems this stubborn cowboy has been fighting the wrong battles the last couple of months." Charlie reached over and touched my knee. "Sorry I let you down, Sadie." He leaned back and closed his eyes for a minute. I figured he kept those tears inside as long as he could. "This changing stuff won't be easy. Can you put up with me?"

I nodded. "Can you stop smoking?"

Charlie reached up into his pocket and handed me the pack. "I already have, Sunshine. I already have."

We gathered up all the cigarettes in the house and broke each one in half before we threw it in the trash can. Charlie even poured the whiskey down the sink. "This probably wouldn't kill me," he said, "but it don't make me very good company."

The next day Charlie went over to Doctor Feldman for a checkup. They told him to chew gum or eat hard candy or peppermints to help with the cravings. Charlie bought a huge bag of lollipops and always had one in his mouth from then on. He joked that he was the lollipop cowboy. Every day he walked around with a rubber ball in his left hand. He sat down and concentrated on squeezing it. Most days he did his other exercises.

Charlie said smoking was harder to give up than he thought. He got grouchy and sometimes yelled when there was no need to, but he didn't yell at me. He slammed around the dishes or kicked at the door as it was swinging shut. He cussed at the television and drank a few too many beers when there was a war movie on NBC. He was a little rough around the edges, but he kept working at it, and he didn't start smoking again. His arm didn't gain that much strength right away, but we were a family, and I worried less and less about it ever changing.

Spring

23

"I got an "A" on my science test today," I said quietly as Mother and Dad and I sat in the living room eating supper on TV trays in front of the TV. They were arguing about whether or not we needed to get a newer pickup because ours hadn't been starting well and was having transmission problems.

"We don't have the money for it," Mother said, as she took a bite of macaroni and cheese.

"Well, I can't afford to miss work again because I can't get that old heap started. Maybe you need to pick up a couple of extra shifts at work?" Dad wiped his face and raised his eyebrows at her.

"Maybe you need to cut back on the cases of beer stacked out in the porch," she said. She looked over at me. "An "A" huh? Well, that's good."

"I got 100%," I said. "I was the only one in the class

to get them all right. We were studying chlorophyll and photosynthesis."

Dad laughed. "Chloro-what?" He rolled his eyes. "They didn't teach that stuff to us in grade school. Of course, you are such a smarty-pants. One hundred percent, huh?" He shook his head and looked back at the TV.

It was quiet again. The light from the TV filled the room with a dim glow. My macaroni and cheese was getting cold, but I wasn't hungry anymore.

24

One Saturday morning at the end of March, I played with Smoke on the living room floor while Charlie read the paper. The telephone rang, and he answered it. I heard him say "You don't say" with that real angry tone of voice. I didn't even need to look; I knew Alice was on the phone.

When I did look over, Charlie stood with his left hand on his hip and his right hand touching his front shirt pocket out of habit. Instead of a cigarette, he found a lollipop and began to unwrap it with his right hand while he cradled the phone with his shoulder. He hadn't had a cigarette in twenty-five days. We kept track on a calendar on the refrigerator. He looked real good and wasn't so grouchy anymore.

"And what do you want me to do, Alice?" Charlie raised his voice, but then he took a breath and lowered it again. "You ain't got no idea what's been going on in Sadie's life because you haven't cared enough to check in. You didn't even give us your phone number the last time you called. What is the matter with you? Yeah. Yeah. I doubt it. Why don't you ask her?"

Charlie looked over at me and motioned with his lollipop to come to the phone. I shook my head "no." I don't know what I was thinking, but all I can say is that I couldn't talk to Alice just then. I didn't want to get my stomach all worked up and starting to think about cardboard boxes. Charlie raised his eyebrows. I shook my head "no," and walked out into the kitchen.

"It seems Sadie is tied up right now, Alice. Guess you get to talk to me."

I grabbed my coat and walked outside. I pulled the inside door shut and let the outside screen door slam and bang against the house a few times. The sound felt good. It was cold and still outside. The sky was clear and bright blue. Sunshine reflected off the glittery snow. I squinted and went out to brush Mercy. I had forgotten my hat and gloves in the house, so I didn't brush her long. Mostly I stood with my hands in my pockets and told her about how I couldn't believe Alice was calling again, and I had no idea what she wanted this time. Mercy nuzzled up against me, warm streams of air shooting out of her nostrils. Her winter coat was thick and long; I was sure she was plenty warm.

Finally, I was too cold to stay out in the barn. When I got back to the house, Charlie was in the kitchen, his head in the oven, scrubbing away. I knew the phone call must have been bad because every time Charlie felt nervous or upset he started cleaning like he was still in the military. The inside of that oven looked like new. His weak arm mostly held a sponge while his strong, right arm did all the work. I sat down at the table and watched him finish rinsing it.

He stood up and stretched. "Want some cocoa? I'll heat some up."

"No, thanks."

Charlie sat down. "Alice wants to see you, Sadie. She thought a visit about Easter would be nice. She wants you to fly there for a couple of days. In fact, she wants me to come too."

My heart skipped a beat. "You too?" I said.

"Yep."

"She don't want me to stay there with her?"

Charlie looked at his hands. "Don't seem so. She said something about not enough room in their little trailer, but a visit would be nice. I don't know what she's up to, but we could check the place out. What do you say?"

I shrugged.

"I called the airlines. We could go two weeks from tomorrow and stay three days. She's your momma, Sadie. She has a right to see you."

I looked up at Charlie. "Do I have to?"

"I don't expect so, but she could come and get you anytime she wants. I figure it's best we try to cooperate. What do you think?"

"Where is she living?"

"Outside Las Vegas, Nevada in a trailer park."

I had never been on an airplane. "How would we get the money for tickets?" I asked.

"I got money. That ain't no problem. She wants to see you. She says she can't afford to come here, and she's got a job, so she can't get the time off. It's up to you, Sadie. It's not up to me to say."

Charlie ordered our tickets and talked to a lawyer in Brookings about all the legal stuff he wanted to discuss with Alice when we were out there. Liza was jealous that I was going to spend spring break in the desert where I could work on a tan. Cal and Kevin agreed to take over the farm chores.

Before I knew it, we were sitting on an airplane, looking down at the frozen prairie like a big old quilt of white and brown and tan squares. Charlie had on new Levis, a white cowboy shirt, and the bolo tie I had given him for Christmas. He looked handsome and nervous. I don't know how many times he reached up for the pocket of his shirt. He didn't have a lollipop for the plane, but chewed on some gum instead.

The day before we left, Liza had painted my fingernails fuchsia pink. I wore the friendship ring she gave me. My hair was very long, and I thought about how different I would look to Alice, how much older. I liked flying. It felt relaxing to have the sound of the motors below me. I realized that my stomach was not all messed up, and considering the trip we were on, I thought that was an amazing thing.

When we landed in Las Vegas, the pilot said it was seventy-four degrees. I could hardly imagine that it was so warm; it was six degrees above zero when we left Sioux Falls. Charlie didn't say much on the flight, but read a *Western Horseman* magazine. When we landed, he turned to me. "You stay right with me every second; we're in the big city now." He even took my hand after we got off the plane. I had held Charlie's hand before, but not very often. His left hand felt pretty strong to me, and he held on and didn't let go until we got down to the baggage area.

Charlie got us a taxi, and we rode through downtown Las Vegas with all the lights and commotion and people. I'd never seen so many blinking lights, and I'd never been in a taxi. Palm trees lined the streets. Houses had sand and gravel for yards, with a small palm tree here and there. There wasn't much green, but there was lots of sunshine. Finally, we got to the trailer park where Alice and Wes lived. We were let out at a small silver and olive-green trailer with curved ends. It reminded me of a giant toaster. I got out of the car and felt a slight curiosity mixed in with my sadness, but the sadness was for having lost my mother. Now, it was a woman named Alice we were going to visit.

She came outside when the taxi drove away.

"Sarah Paul! Oh my, look at you!" Alice had on a tank top and shorts. She was real tan, her hair looked blonder than ever, and she wore lots of make-up. She held a cigarette in one hand and reached around and hugged me with her other hand, the one that held her drink. I stood there holding my suitcase. "You have grown a foot, girl! I swear! A good twelve inches at least." She looked over at Charlie and smiled what looked like a sincere smile. "Hello, Charlie. Thank you so much for bringing my baby out to see me!"

Charlie nodded. "Hello, Alice."

There was an uncomfortable pause. Alice took a sip of her drink. "Why don't you all come in for awhile? Come on in and have a drink." She opened the door while she had the cigarette in her mouth and motioned for me to go first. "Wes is at work right now, but you'll get to see him later. He's got a new job that he likes pretty good. Hours are better than some. Charlie, what will you have?"

"You got a beer?"

Alice nodded and Charlie looked relieved. The trailer was small and full of rust and olive-green furniture. The plaid sofa took up most of the living area and there was a chair to match. There were mirrors on the living room wall and the kitchen cupboards. It was dark and smelled musty.

"You got a lot of mirrors," I said, trying to think of some way to push away the silence.

"Yeah, they're supposed to make the place look bigger. It's kind of small, but it works okay for two people for now. 'Course we ain't planning on staying here long term or nothing." Alice smiled and looked over at me. "So tell me all about everything, Sugar Plum." She smiled, like we were best friends having a chat. Like we were sitting on the bed and having a slumber party. And her calling me Sugar Plum.

"What do you want to know?" I asked. I tried hard to be nice and not get angry like Charlie told me.

"Oh, tell me about school, friends, whatever. How do you like living in South Dakota?"

I found this game confusing. What was I suppose to say? I wanted to ask her the questions. Why hadn't she called me more often and asked then how I liked South Dakota? How was school going? Did I need anything? Did I want anything? Did I miss her? Was there anything she could do?

Instead, I cleared my throat. "School's good. I got some friends. Charlie takes real good care of me."

I looked up at Alice and she looked at the floor. Then I looked at Charlie. His eyes said I didn't have to worry so much about what I said. His eyes told me everything was going to be okay. Then he winked and smiled.

"Where are you working now, Alice?" he asked.

Alice looked up and got perky again. "At the Stardust on the strip. I cash in chips, do a little waitressing, some of this, some of that. Pretty good pay, but it don't seem to go too far." She looked over at Charlie as she lit another cigarette. "You ain't had a cigarette since you got here. Did you run out?" She reached out her pack to offer him one.

"No, thanks. I quit."

"Well, I'll be." Alice shrugged and smiled. "You still like your hamburger grilled till it's crispy, don't you Sarah Paul?"

"People call me Sadie now."

"I'm sorry." Alice looked a little nervous, and suddenly I felt real guilty.

"I like them that way," I said. "My hamburgers."

. . .

We sat around talking about the weather and the terrible blizzards we had back in South Dakota. Alice kept drinking her scotch and water, but Charlie switched to ice tea after a beer. I drank Coke and played solitaire with a deck of cards I found on the coffee table. Wes came back later, and we had a barbecue. He talked mostly to Alice and Charlie and that was fine by me. I didn't have anything to say to that man anyway.

After supper, Alice said, "I'll drive you two over to a motel that's near where I work. It's pretty cheap for the area, and it has a pool."

"I didn't bring along a swimming suit anyway," I said.

"Well, you and I better run over to Sears first to get you one. Come on Sugar Plum."

I figured she couldn't bring herself to call me Sadie, since it hadn't been her idea. Since it didn't have anything to do with her. Since I came up with it after she pushed me out of her life.

In the car, she asked me how everything was going. "I told you. Everything's fine," I said.

"You like it all right there?"

"Yep."

"You mad at me?"

I sighed. I felt older than my own mother. "No, Alice, I ain't mad at you anymore."

"Why are you calling me Alice?" She started to cry. "I'm still you mother, Sarah. I am the one who gave birth to you. Don't forget that."

"I won't if you don't," I said, half under my breath.

She bought me a blue and green two-piece swimsuit, a pair of sandals, and two pair of shorts. I knew what she was trying to do, but I liked the clothes, and I said thanks.

We went back and picked up Charlie. He looked glad to see me. Alice was running late for work, so she dropped us and our suitcases at the office of the Thunder Mountain Motel. When Charlie asked for two rooms, I was a little surprised. I knew it was a lot of money, and we couldn't really afford it. I tugged on his sleeve. "Could I maybe sleep in your room? I'm kind of scared to sleep in a motel room all by myself," I said.

Charlie nodded, as if he hadn't thought of that. "Make it one room with two beds, I guess," he told the desk clerk.

25

The next morning, Charlie decided to meet Alice for breakfast after her shift. He said the talking they needed to do was best done without me. "Will you be all right here by yourself?" he asked.

"Sure." The pool was right by the office, which had a glass wall, so I could see the desk clerk if I had any trouble. "I think I'll go swimming."

"Sounds like a good idea, but don't you go talking to no strangers and keep that room key with you at all times."

"Yes, sir." I smiled.

Charlie smiled back. "What do you think of this old desert gambling paradise?"

"I don't care for it much, but it's nice to get a break from the snow."

"Yeah, it's a sandy, dirty old piece of property if you ask me. I'll be back in a couple of hours. Maybe I'll make some plans for us with your momma for later. Have a good swim." Charlie had on another nice cowboy shirt. He checked his hat in the mirror, tucked a manila envelope full of legal papers under his arm and left.

The sun was already high enough in the sky to feel hot, and after the long cold winter, it felt wonderful. I wasn't much of a swimmer, but I loved to go under the water and hold my breath until it felt like my lungs would burst. My long hair waved around my face, and I imagined I was a mermaid in the South Seas. Then I would push to the surface and gasp for air, feeling that sudden rush of energy like I was refueling.

I was watching game shows on the TV when Charlie got back. He had been gone a good couple of hours.

"You look a little pink. Guess you got enough sun for one day." Charlie put his hat on the side table. "How was the pool?"

"Good. How was Alice?"

Charlie chuckled. "Same old Alice."

I was going to wait him out, but I felt my stomach starting to revolt and decided I would do whatever I could to keep it from turning inside out. "So what did you two talk about? Tell me everything. She . . ." I couldn't get any more words out.

Charlie reached over and turned off the TV. "First of all, Alice was hoping I could give her a loan. Seems her gambling itch is getting scratched a bit too often. Things are a little tight right now. We discussed that possibility, and I let her know I wasn't one bit anxious to go down that road. Then we talked about you."

Charlie paused, as if trying to figure out the right way to say what was on his mind. I could hardly stand it. "Charlie you better just tell me before I have to go in that bathroom and throw up because I can't take this too well."

Charlie looked over at me and then at his polished boots. My stomach told me it was too late, and I headed for the bathroom. It was only the dry heaves, since there wasn't much in my stomach to throw up but some pretzels I'd bought in the vending machine by the pool. Charlie didn't come in, and I felt so sure that my life was getting back on that crazy rollercoaster, I let anger work its way in next to that fear. I washed my face and walked back into the bedroom with my hands on my hips. "She wants me back, don't she? She expects me to stay here in this hole and live in that tin can with her and . . ."

"No."

". . . Wes the weasel. I don't want to stay; my home is with --" I looked over at Charlie and he looked so sad. "No?"

"No."

"She doesn't want me to stay?" I felt a rush of relief, before I started wondering why Charlie looked so sad.

"Don't you. . . don't you want me, Charlie?"

"Of course I do, Sadie. I'd do anything for you, you know that."

"Then why do you look so disappointed?"

"I'm disappointed in your mother. I am sorry I have to tell you that you are not convenient for her. I can't imagine anyone being able to walk away from any child, let alone you."

I sat back down on my bed. "So you're going to take me back with you?"

"I bought you a two-way ticket, Sadie. I never intended to leave you here, at least not without a fight."

"What about all them papers?" I asked.

"She signed them. She said I could have legal guardianship. Of course that don't mean she don't have legal rights and could claim you anytime she wanted. We got it notarized. It's all legal. We don't know where your daddy is, but I don't expect he'll ever give us any trouble since he's never paid a penny to your upbringing since he left."

"So what now?"

"Looks like you're stuck with this old cowboy."

"Looks like we're stuck with each other," I said. I sat down on the bed. "Can we go home now?"

Charlie laughed. "Sounds good to me, but we got a

flight out tomorrow. Your momma went home to get some sleep. She wants us to meet her for supper at a place near here. Some fancy buffet, I guess. All the food you can eat. Speaking of food, I bet you're about ready for some lunch."

My stomach settled down quickly. I could feel a low growl. "Yeah, all I had today was some pretzels."

"Let's go get you some grub, and then maybe we'll catch a matinee somewhere to kill some time."

That evening we ate supper with my mother, and for the first time in a long time, I felt good about my connection to her. I guess because she let me go back to South Dakota, I was able to forgive her for wanting me to go.

I told her about how Liza and I rode Mercy bareback all over the farm. I told her about Smoke and her little bed in my room. I told her about Ms. Jamison and how someday I might be a writer. She smiled and looked happier than I could remember. It was an easy gift to give, letting her in on my life. I figured if she kept in touch with me, I could keep her updated on what it was like to live normal, like a family. I thought maybe someday she would like to try it too.

26

Dear Mother,

How are things with you? It is almost spring here. Charlie says we are about out of the woods. He likes to talk like that about the weather. He even screams at the ceiling and tells Old Man Winter to get lost. He can be real funny sometimes.

School is going well. My grades are good. Ms. Jamison, my English teacher, says that I have a good imagination and a talent for putting my feelings on paper. She says I should keep up my writing over the summer, and she would be happy to read it in the fall, so I figured I would practice some by writing letters. You don't need to answer or anything, if you don't have time, but I can tell you about things around here.

It is still cold outside, so the horses are all in the barn most of the time. We have a cute new colt. She is pitch-black with one white sock. I call her River, but I don't think that will be her name. Charlie is planning to sell her before fall, so I am trying not to get too attached. She does seem to like me though; she comes right up to me when we feed the horses. You should see her; she is so small.

Mercy is doing fine. I just got back from a long ride with Charlie. There is so much snow, and the horses' legs sink down into it, but Mercy doesn't seem to mind. I think she likes the exercise and the chance to get out of the barn and take a look around. She follows Charlie's horse right along, so it is easy to know where to go. I am getting better at riding. Charlie even says so. This summer I want to ride Mercy to town to visit my best friend, Liza. Charlie says if I stay off the highway it should be okay.

Well, I better be going. I have some homework to finish before I go to bed. I will write again soon.

Love,

Sadie

Epilogue

The snow stayed around that spring until almost the end of April. Charlie said most years the tulips were already done blooming, but we still had dirty drifts piled up between the barn and the silo, and all the ditches were half-full of old snow. At least the roads were open, and I could go to school and see my friends.

By the end of May, the sun was hot and the lilacs were blooming at the end of the house, sending out that sweet perfume. I was done with the seventh grade. Liza and I made lots of plans for the summer. We were going to take swimming lessons at the pool in Brookings. She was going to ride her bike out to our house some days, and I was going to ride Mercy into town if Charlie would let me. We planned sleepovers and shopping trips to Sioux Falls with her mom. Charlie told me I could help drive the tractor again to pick up bales. He said if I started doing some regular chores around the farm, he would start giving me an allowance. I imagined what I would do with some money of my own.

The first day of June, I packed a lunch and rode Mercy down to the creek. Charlie was busy fixing some fence on the corral. He said that as long as I stayed on the section I would be fine. He told me to be home by four o'clock.

The ditches were all dry, and the grass was long. Mercy liked to walk down in the bed of the ditch, so I always had to be careful no big branches or junk was there to trip her up. Charlie said Eugene Rasmussen mowed these ditches for hay, so they would be clean. I still worried about Mercy stepping on a bottle or an old tin can and getting cut.

Mercy walked along as if she was as pleased as I was to be out in the sunshine and free of responsibilities. The air was full of the smells of late spring. Apple trees were in blossom. I could almost smell the grass growing and the earth drying up after the hard winter.

Elbow Creek was at the end of the mile, and there was a little bridge over the road. Mercy and I went down into the wide ditch where I tied her to one of the fence posts. She liked the thick green grass down by the creek.

I sat down near her and threw dandelions into the rushing water. A meadowlark landed in a big old cottonwood tree across the creek.

It was a perfect day. I watched the lazy clouds and imagined what they were as they slowly changed shapes. I imagined one was a covered wagon, and I was a pioneer crossing the prairie for the first time. I imagined that Mercy pulled my wagon, and that my wagon was full of my cardboard boxes. But unlike the past, when I thought about the boxes, they were just boxes. My stomach didn't dance the crazy dance of worry.

I was relaxed. I was home. I lay back in the sweet grass and imagined I was a native to this place. I was someone who had always been a part of the land, and the land was a part of me. The sky was above me: big, blue, and full of promise. I thought about all that. I thought about how warm the sun felt on my face, and I smiled because I knew it was all true.

About the Author

Kathleen Patrick is a poet and fiction writer who grew up on the prairies of the Midwest, riding horses, jumping rope, hula hooping, and writing poetry. Her bestselling book, *Airmail: A Story of War in Poems*, centers on her family's experience with wars, from the Vietnam War to the present. *Mercy*, her first novel, is a coming-of-age story set in 1970 on the plains of South Dakota. *Anxiety in the Wilderness* is her first collection of short stories. *Perfume River,* a novel for adults, is a story about anxiety and hope, about believing in the future and reconciling the past. *The Shoe Box Waltz* is a cautionary tale about two young women in search of adventure. It is her fifth book.

Please Review This Book!

Reviews help authors more than you might think. Sometimes they even help readers decide what to read. If you liked *Mercy*, please consider writing a review and sharing it where ever you bought the book. It can be a few words or a few short sentences. I would greatly appreciate it.

Free Short Story!

Sign up for my mailing list at the address below and get a free short story! "Anxiety in the Wilderness" is the title story from my recent collection of short stories by the same title.

https://patrickpoetry.com/

Also by Kathleen Patrick

Airmail: A Story of War in Poems

Anxiety in the Wilderness

Perfume River

The Shoe Box Waltz

Words and Reviews

Airmail: A Story of War in Poems

"I read it in one sitting and thoroughly enjoyed (if that's the right word) every poem." — Tim O'Brien, author of *The Things They Carried*

"*Airmail: A Story of War in Poems*...is a great example of how letters and conversations can be turned into stunning poetry. Patrick shares the words and thoughts of seven uncles who served in the military, five of them in Southeast Asia during the American war in Vietnam. ...It's always cool to see letters sent home from war turned into poems. They become letters from America sent back to America. Kathleen Patrick shows us what it can look like when it's done poetically and done right." — Bill McCloud, The VVA Veteran magazine

"Love the voice and reading pace. It's great, and the content is amazing. I am a Vietnam vet and I can relate 100%. Thanks for taking the time to do this project." — J.I.

"Some very strong work here, grounded in correspondence that Kathleen had with her uncles while they served in Vietnam, and also in their correspondence with their parents, subsequent interviews, etc. An amazing piece of work. This is the best war

lit I have read since *The Things they Carried* by Tim O'Brien."
— P.L.

"A story that stays with you. I read a lot of historical fiction surrounding WWI and II, but this collection of poems highlighting the perspectives of a family living through Vietnam was just as beautiful. Reading poetry framed as letters by young men wanting to serve and the loved ones they left behind was powerfully written and even more powerful in the things that were left unsaid. This is a collection that should be read slowly, absorbing the words from each letter. — A. C.

"Wow...Honestly, I don't read a lot of poetry and didn't think I would like it. However, I loved it; it sucked me right in, and I thought it was beautifully done." — L.M.

"This collection distills so much family history into consumable little poems that will leave you wrecked in the best possible way. A beautiful read." — H.C.

"*Airmail: A Story of War in Poems* is a book about going off to war, a book about coming back home, and a book about those who are left behind." — Kathleen Patrick

Mercy

"*Mercy* is a phenomenal young adult coming of age story that will capture the hearts of readers of all ages!"—K.C.

"*Mercy* is a story of adolescence, but adults would love it as well.

It explores the emotional turbulence inherent in dysfunctional families and what it takes to move from dysfunction to love to mercy. Any book that can make me cry and laugh out loud is a winner. *Mercy* is a winner!"—J.C.

"A coming of age, found family, young adult novel. A heartwarming story about a twelve-year-old girl named Sadie who finds the family she always craved in her uncle on a farm. After Sadie's mother struggles with gambling addiction after her father's departure, Sadie has a life of instability and worry. Great short read. The only thing I have to say bad about the story is that it simply isn't long enough!"—K.F.

"Mercy was just a great story and a breath of fresh air!" — L.P.

"Mercy is a story about compassion and kindness. It celebrates the idea families can come in all shapes and sizes and consists of people who support one another, even when it isn't easy. It is a story that reverberates with the basic human need to be loved."
—Kathleen Patrick

Anxiety in the Wilderness

"A book of short stories that can only be described as bittersweet. Some parts defiantly pulled at my heartstrings. The author herself said the book was written over a long time period. This comes across in the different scenarios in which the characters are involved in. Each a little exceptional tale of it's own. I especially liked the crossover of characters. I am now patiently waiting for a full novel set in the Iowa wilderness!" — K. F., Goodreads review

"The poetic language of the stories lends a warmth to the storytelling that helps to bring the characters to life. Each story describes a different human worry or anxiety that we all may have experienced at some point in our lives; therefore, each story is relatable in its own way....Short stories are a disappearing art form, and Patrick demonstrates why we should keep them around. There is no grandiosity of language that detracts from the storyline or from the artful character descriptions. Characters navigate their way through their predicaments one day at a time. The poignant vignettes showcase the rawness of various human emotions, much like a snapshot of an expert photographer. " —B. M., Goodreads Review

"I loved this book! From beginning to end the characters smack of realism and you can see people you know or yourself in them. I wish it were the first book I a series of ten — because I wanted more!"

Perfume River

"It is a beautifully written novel with deep feelings. It is the kind of book that wins prizes." E.S.,

"The characters are well drawn, and the story is both touching and humorous. Worth the read!" E.S.

"Patrick's prose is smooth, even, and consistent. As with her other work, her use of words is sparse and succinct leaving the reader to indulge in their own imaginings of the space and events. The pauses and silences are evocative." J.S.

"Absolutely loved the main character! Great read!" K. K.

"I enjoy Kathleen Patrick's concise descriptive abilities

sprinkled with emotional and intellectual truths." CT